LOVING HOPE

MILITARY ROMANCE — WITH A SCIENCE FICTION EDGE

ANN GIMPEL

Edited by ANGELA KELLY

Edited by DIANE EAGLE

Illustrated by FIONA JAYDE

CONTENTS

LOVING HOPE

GENTECH REBELLION, BOOK FOUR

Military Romance
(with a science fiction edge)
By
Ann Gimpel

COPYRIGHT PAGE

Hope's had her eye on Charlie for a long time, for all the good it's done her. He's not even aware of her existence—other than as a fellow agent working Black Ops for the CIA. Her friends, Glory, Honor, and Charity, found men to love, so Hope knows it's possible. But the odds aren't in her favor. Not in a world of normal humans where she's a genetically modified aberration. Hell, even she refers to her kind as freaks. What man in his right mind would want one of those in his bed?

Charlie swore off women after his last marriage went down in drama-tipped flames fifteen years ago. His first mistress is danger. He fell in love with the adrenaline rush when he signed on as a Navy Seal right out of college, and he never got over the thrill of pitting himself against the impossible.

Hope caught his eye the night she escaped her compound, but years of ignoring anything resembling a feeling made it easy to ignore the attraction—until they're paired on a mission. Her intelligence and resourcefulness impress the hell out of him, but her half-naked body, exposed after an animal attack, forces him to face feelings he was certain he'd buried for good.

CHAPTER 1

*H*ope blinked dirt out of her eyes and stifled a groan. She didn't want to risk an energy flare looking for the others. Doing anything other than keeping her resources muffled was an enormous risk.

She took a mouthful of water from the canteen hanging off her field belt and swished it around her mouth. Time had passed since a blast hit her helicopter, knocking it out of the air. Maybe as much as an hour. Things happened fast after the bird was hit, and her team leader, Charlie McClaren, folded her hand around the ripcord on her parachute.

He'd all but pushed her out the open chopper door with exhortations to, "Watch out for the rotor, goddammit."

A few other choice instructions were lost in the slipstream as she plummeted from the dying aircraft, her pounding heart stenciling fear from her head to her toes.

What was supposed to be a simple out-and-back mission had turned into something much more complex, never mind much more dangerous. She'd been expecting Charlie or Frank to materialize ever since she cut herself out of the tree her chute got tangled in, but neither man showed up.

She didn't understand why. They couldn't have landed very far away after the crash—assuming they made it out of the chopper intact. Too rattled by her first actual parachute jump, she'd neglected to watch for the other chutes, which would've told her the location of her teammates.

Were they dead? Or tripped up by the old growth forest?

She'd been careful chopping her way out of a particularly tall tree. Her caution ate up well over half an hour while she freed herself from where she swung thirty feet above the ground. She picked splinters out of her hands as she considered what to do next.

According to the GPS in her augmented brain, she was in a wooded corridor in north central Maine. She, Charlie, and Frank had been on a routine mission to pick up Cortexiphan, an experimental drug banned by the FDA, from a freak compound near Bangor. Not that they'd expected the freaks—a renegade group of genetically modified humans who wanted to take down the U.S. government—to just hand over the drug, but military planes had annihilated the settlement. No one expected it would be difficult to waltz in and locate the chemical.

Hope shook her head. Underestimating her people was always a mistake. The genetically modified were smarter, stronger, faster, and more capable of pivoting in response to adverse conditions than normal humans ever dreamed of being.

She sheltered in a thick grove of some sort of deciduous tree and leaned against one of them. Could she risk her communicator? Would telepathy be safer? Hope grimaced. Freaks had to be behind the attack on her chopper, which meant nothing was safe. Who else would shoot down a CIA chopper over U.S. soil?

She bit hard on her lower lip. She understood freaks—how they thought, what made them tick—because she was one. She'd escaped the compounds, though, and left that life behind.

"What do I do now?"

She started at the sound of her voice, not realizing she'd spoken aloud until she heard the words. A quick glance at the sky told her she didn't have much daylight left to work with. Not that it mattered. She could always dial in her night vision, but it held a particular energy signature.

The flash of warmth in Charlie's hazel eyes as he'd covered her hand with his, instructing her how to yank the ripcord, filled her mind. She liked him. A lot. But he barely knew she existed beyond her working under him. She'd made a few pathetic attempts at flirting, but he'd ignored her. Maybe her shy smiles were so subtle he hadn't interpreted them the way she hoped, but that probably wasn't it. She was a freak. He was a normal human, and a goddamned good-looking one at that. He could have his pick of women. No reason on earth to look twice at her.

Much like the genetically altered men she'd spent her life with, Charlie was tall and rangy, with dark hair and hazel eyes. He was addicted to danger the same as all CIA operatives. When twin fires burned in the backs of his eyes, it was all she could do not to throw herself into his arms and beg him to take her.

Here.

Now.

In front of everyone.

She tossed her head, muffling a snort. She knew next to nothing about men, sex, or love. Her entire primer on all things human was derived from hours of television and the Internet. Her other source of information came from pumping Honor, Glory, and Charity, three of her closest friends, about their relationships with CIA agents they'd hooked up with.

A branch crackled behind her. Hope lunged for her sidearm, thought better of it, and focused her mental kinetics. She didn't loose anything—not yet. Power ran through her in high voltage jolts. Holding it in abeyance wasn't easy, but she needed to know what she faced. The minute she targeted someone, her ability would glow like a beacon, alerting any genetically modified human in the area to both her presence and precise location.

"Hope! I've been hunting for you ever since the chopper crashed."

Frank limped from behind a bush. He was well over six feet tall with heavy slabs of muscle providing superior physical abilities. Genetically modified like her, his shaggy dark hair brushed his shoulders, and his amber animal-like eyes with vertical slit pupils came close to radiating joy. Given Frank's taciturn ways, that said a lot.

She siphoned off the lethal force dancing through her body an electron at a time. "Fuck!" She trotted to his side. "I almost killed you."

A crooked grin lent him a boyish appearance. "I felt the energy build. Figured I needed to say something."

Hope took a closer look. A wicked looking gash ran from below Frank's right eye to his cheekbone, and his hands were abraded and bleeding. She ran a hand down his body, scanning for injuries.

Before she was done, he batted it away. "I twisted my ankle when I landed in a bramble thicket. It's how I got so banged up—fighting my way out of thorns as long as my thumb. I've instituted a healing program. Should be better than new in a few hours." Breath hissed from between his teeth. "Shit! After my last impromptu exit from a chopper, I promised myself I'd practice parachuting, but somehow I never freed up the time."

"Yeah, well, I've never even come close to doing anything like jumping out of a helicopter. Didn't like it much. Any idea where Charlie is?"

Frank shook his head. "I was hoping he'd be with you."

"We may not have had all that fancy commando training, but I never would've guessed how easy it is to lose someone between an auto-rotating helicopter and the ground."

"We have to locate him." Frank narrowed his eyes, or he might have winced, she couldn't tell. "You haven't expended any power, or I'd have found you sooner. Charlie certainly hasn't used any."

"It's not safe. Charlie must've figured that out." She crossed her arms under her breasts. "Freaks did this, huh?"

He cocked his head to one side. "Who else? I'm surprised you asked. Their signature is all over it."

Hope shrugged, feeling uncomfortable for missing something obvious. "Maybe it is. Once the chopper started going nuts, I kind of stopped thinking."

He looked at her then. Really looked and ran his own scan of her systems before she could move out of range.

"I'm all right." She took a few steps away. "If I weren't, I'd have told you."

"Needed to check for myself," he said gruffly. "We have more latitude with two of us—but only if we're able to tap into all of our abilities."

"What's that supposed to mean?" She frowned, still not feeling a hundred percent.

His face settled into the patronizing lines she associated with Nameless Ones, genetically modified men who'd made her life hell when they lived in compounds. All of them—men and women alike —were products of genetic research originally hatched up by the U.S. government. Appalled by how they were treated, they staged a rebellion, and blew up the breeding farms. While women had been an integral part of the rebellion, they'd been relegated to second-class citizenry after a few years of living in hidden compounds. Their abilities were superior to the men's, and the men had been frightened of losing the upper hand—

"It means we need to risk exposure to find Charlie. We can't leave without him." Frank's words broke into her thoughts, and she shelved her foray into the past.

Hope set her jaw in determination and moved back to Frank's side, so she could join her mental energy with his more easily. "Ready."

"Before we do something that's certain to compromise us, have you looked for him?"

"Not really. My chute got stuck in a tree, and it took a ridiculous amount of time to free myself. I was just getting my bearings and deciding what to do next when you showed up."

Frank made a chopping motion with one hand. "Enough. I don't need the long version."

The same anger she always felt when a Nameless One got heavy handed flared hot and bright. "You don't run things anymore. Stop ordering me around." She curled one hand into a fist and punched the air in his direction.

"I wasn't—" His nostrils flared with annoyance, but he bit off the rest of his sentence. "Never mind. You're already in my head. We'll do a short, fast scan. Thirty seconds tops."

A frisson of apprehension ran down her spine. What if Charlie were dead?

He can't be. He just can't.

Why not? Men in his line of work die all the time...

"Hope!" Frank's voice cut like a bullwhip. "I don't give a fuck how you feel about him. Help me do this."

Heat blotched her chest and face. "Sorry," she mumbled. "Told you before that I was ready, and I still am."

"On my count. One. Two. Three."

Hope shot energy in tandem with Frank's. Relief filled her when Charlie's unique energy indicator pinged back clean and pure. "Yes!" She pumped the air with her already fisted hand.

Frank shot an odd glance her way. "He's alive," he said slowly.

The same clammy uneasiness she'd felt before they looked settled across her shoulders like a yoke, and she made a come along gesture with two fingers. "Whatever it is. Spill it."

"He's in a compound."

"What?" Hope wasn't sure she'd heard right. "Didn't we bomb the fuck out of the one up here?"

"One of them, yeah." Frank drew his brows into a thick, worried line. "There's another about a mile from our current position. Apparently that one's still online and functional."

She reached for her wrist computer, intent on radioing Langley to send reinforcements, but Frank shook his head. "Why not?" She chewed her lower lip. "We can't take on a whole compound by ourselves."

"If we radio for help, they'll hear. If they're on the fence about killing Charlie, it could send them over the edge and sign his death warrant."

She unclenched her fist and flexed her fingers, forcing order out of the chaos her mind had become. "Langley will know something's wrong. They'll have tracked our craft with radar."

"Yes, and they'll know we're no longer in the air. Them sending assistance without us asking for it isn't a problem."

"Tell me what you're thinking." She batted back a frantic need to storm the freaks' fortress and kill the men one by one. Anything to get Charlie out of their clutches alive.

Frank shifted to closely shielded telepathic speech. *"It's a long shot, but what I think might work is..."*

CHARLIE MANHANDLED Hope to get her outside the chopper. He recognized the wild look in her eyes and kicked himself roundly for not prioritizing exit training for all the women on his team. Frank was another story. He'd adopted a stoic expression and stepped past Charlie into open air.

Intuition on overdrive, Charlie followed his people, tapping a coded distress message through his wrist computer after he deployed his chute. HQ might not pick it up right away, but it wasn't the end of the world. He liked it when the other side turned up the heat. It kept things interesting. Besides, the CIA would figure out their bird wasn't airborne soon enough. In the meantime, maybe he could find a freak or two to grill for data.

Veteran of hundreds of jumps, Charlie twisted sideways and slipped handily through the forest canopy. He rolled to the ground, gathering his chute almost before he had his feet under him. Folding and stuffing on autopilot, he figured he'd survey his surroundings then locate Frank and Hope.

Hope.

Warmth flared at the thought of her. Hell, more than warmth. The woman was hotter than a boatload of Sirens with her long, dark hair and cat-green eyes. Tall, like all the genetically modified women, her shapely form mixed muscle with curves in the right places. His body came alive as he pictured her, but he told it to stand down. No matter how sensual Hope was, it didn't matter. He was done with females. They only got in the way. He'd never had a relationship where they didn't start trying to change him as soon as he took them to bed. It was subtle at first but became more strident when he ignored their cues. He'd been married once. Never again.

His bachelor status and Black Ops lifestyle played hell with his sex life, but the freedom was worth it.

He shouldered his pack with the chute folded inside and sent a short blast of energy outward, surveying his surroundings. He'd taken a series of injections to make himself more like the freaks. While using his augmented power wasn't exactly second nature, he'd gotten more comfortable with it over time.

His power slapped back at him so hard his ears rang, and he did a double take. That had never happened before. What the fuck?

Slowly, more cautious this time, he paid out energy, seeking the characteristic pings that belonged to humans versus freaks versus animal life. Answers bombarded him, and adrenaline poured through his system. He raised his AK-47 to his shoulder and scanned the thick tree cover for the enemy.

His finger flirted with the trigger. Were Hope and Frank close enough to wound or kill with a stray bullet? He hadn't sensed them. What nearly mowed him down was the realization he was surrounded by at least twenty freaks. Maybe twenty-five.

Fuck! Crap! Goddammit!

He tightened his fingers around the gun. If he didn't mount

offensive action damned fast, the freaks would take him out. He pushed his power wide open, seeking his people. An odd sensation hit him right between the eyes. He fought it, but the rifle dropped from his hands, and his knees buckled. His back bowed painfully just before darkness hit him like a sledgehammer.

~

POUNDING temples brought Charlie jolting back to consciousness. His head hurt like a bitch. He wanted to rub it and jerked a hand upward only to have it stop. A cuff tightened painfully around his wrist, and he lowered his arm.

He forced his eyes open and twisted his head from side to side. It made the pain worse, but he had to know if he had anything to work with. He lay on his back on a thin pallet spread over a concrete floor. His wrists were cuffed to bolts set in the concrete, but his ankles were free. The room was rectangular and small. Light filtered in through a window covered with a torn shade. Beyond his pallet, the space was empty. A stout wooden door was set into the far wall. Metal staves crisscrossed along its length.

Charlie scooted his butt back and adopted a bent over seated position. Freaks had shot down his chopper. It had to be retribution for the CIA knocking out several of their compounds. Regardless of their motives, they'd set a net and captured him. He made a sideways chopping motion to free one hand, but got nowhere. He hadn't expected it to work, but being helpless wasn't his style.

Christ!

Were Frank and Hope somewhere in this building right along with him? He pushed his mind voice outward, but it exploded in his head. Spots danced in front of his eyes, and he bit back a muffled yelp of pain. It felt as if someone were slicing through his head right behind his eyes with a buzz saw.

He took shallow breaths until he had the upper hand again. He'd be goddamned if he'd turn into a whimpering ninny because of a little discomfort. He took stock of his situation. No telepathy; that was abundantly clear. No wrist computer. Naturally, they'd taken it. Also no rifle, no sidearm, no knives, no communicator, no sat phone.

Focus! There's always a way. I have to find it.

What could he do? He'd been in almost the same situation in the Middle East—not dealing with genetically altered men, but with Al Qaida, who were almost as bad in some respects, and much worse in others. They wrote the book where *ruthless* was concerned. The freaks were pikers by comparison.

Charlie forced himself to breathe. To think. He had an opportunity since they'd left him alone, clearly convinced he was toast. He was an engineer by trade. He'd majored in aeronautical engineering before he joined the Navy Seals and put in three tours in the Middle East. It was where he met Milton, who convinced him to sign on with the CIA. That had been a few years ago, and he'd never looked back.

He focused on the cuffs, recognizing them as an older style that gave way to determined probing. He pawed through the pockets he could reach, seeking something as simple as a paperclip, but without success. Pain throbbed from his lower lip. He'd bitten so hard on it, he'd drawn blood.

Licking away the salty substance, an idea took shape. He couldn't use his power to project anything beyond the ten by twelve foot room he'd been tossed into, but maybe he could marshal it on a local basis.

He focused a thin thread of kinetics at one of the cuffs, ready to draw back the second it boomeranged on him, but it never happened. The cuff warmed, and then became uncomfortably hot. Smoke rose, and the stench of his own flesh burning filled his nostrils.

"Come on, you motherfucker," he growled. "Open."

Maybe it was the words, but his right cuff popped its catch. Charlie didn't waste time savoring his victory. He repeated his actions on the left cuff and sprang to his feet the moment it loosened. He eyed the door, but discarded it immediately. If the freaks had posted a guard, he'd be in the corridor.

Silent as a panther, he sidled to the side of the window and twitched the shade aside. His eyes widened. The goddamned window had a latch. How could the freaks have been so stupid?

Because they never thought I could free myself.

Maybe they don't know I had the injections to make me more like them.

Charlie worked as efficiently as he could. Fast and quiet would get him out of here. A glance told him he was in a ground level room. Piece of cake. He jimmied the sash and waited, barely breathing.

Nothing.

No patrols, no foot traffic outside what had to be a compound. He recalled the master map of the compound locations, but reeled himself in before that exercise went very far. He had no idea where he was. He could've been out for hours, and they might've moved him a long way from where they'd shot his bird out of the sky.

Didn't matter.

He let himself out the window and crouched on the ground, scanning everything he could see. Once he was convinced he had a clear shot, he made for the surrounding woods. Time enough to sort things out from there.

The important thing was he was free. This was the USA, not the hinterlands of Iraq or Afghanistan. All he had to do was find a dwelling and put in a call to Langley. Even if Frank and Hope were being held prisoner, there wasn't much he could do as a solo operative to free them without weapons or ammunition.

No. His best bet—and their best chance for survival—was calling in reinforcements as fast as he could. Ignoring what felt like knives cutting through his temples from the headache that hadn't abated much, he slid from tree to tree until he'd put half a mile between him and the compound. By then his head felt a little better, and he broke into a jog, navigating via the augmented programming in his mind. He wasn't as competent as a full-blooded freak, but he was better than before the injections.

Much better.

A straight line heading west should bring him to farms that dotted this part of Maine, and sooner rather than later. Charlie put his head down and ran for all he was worth. His team needed him, and he'd do his damnedest to ensure their survival.

CHAPTER 2

Hope trotted next to Frank, keeping to thick undergrowth rather than a road, which would have made their journey faster and easier. Worry for Charlie ate at her, but Frank's plan had slightly better than a fifty-fifty chance of success. She'd run the probabilities several times. Highest she'd come up with was fifty-eight percent. Lowest was fifty-one.

She sent a quick blast of kinetics, more to reassure herself than anything else that the freaks holding Charlie hadn't killed him. Nothing bounced back. Her stomach tightened into an uncomfortable knot. She pushed energy outward again, slowing her pace to make certain the effort received all of her attention.

Frank skidded to a halt and wrapped a hand around her upper arm. "What the fuck are you doing?" he growled. "So far no one knows we're here, and I'd like to keep it that way for as long as—"

Hope wrenched away from him and spun so she stood toe to toe with the Nameless One. "Charlie's gone. I can't sense him." She clung to outrage and fury so she wouldn't fold into a messy heap on the ground with her arms wrapped around herself, trying not to cry.

"Oh for the love of God." Frank grabbed her again and shook her before letting go. "Of course you can't sense him. Freaks have him in a shielded room. They want to drain every last bit of data they can out of him. For that, they need time. It's not in their best interest to stow Charlie somewhere he could be easily found."

Frank stopped to inhale noisily. "They probably don't know he's had the injections to make him more like them, but they will have found the location chips the CIA embedded under his skin at the back of his neck."

Hope closed her teeth over her lower lip hard. Pain helped her focus. "Why not just rip them out of him?"

Frank sent an incredulous glance skittering her way. "Really? Like that would be easier than dumping him in a shielded room? You're not thinking, Hope. Use that augmented programming. You're reasoning like a woman, not a soldier."

She bristled. "How would you have any idea how women solve problems?"

Frank turned away without answering and loped toward their objective. Hope fell in behind him. "Your plan has holes in it. And they just got a whole lot bigger. I haven't run new probabilities, but—"

"Yeah," he broke in, his voice gruff. "I know. If you don't like it, come up with something better."

"What makes you think the freaks are going to believe you when you beg them to take you back into the fold? Even if they do, and it buys me time to discover Charlie's location, how the fuck do I do that if they have him sequestered somewhere my kinetics can't penetrate?"

"The answer to your first question is we've always been shy of genetic researchers. They might not want me back, but they'd be worse than fools to refuse me. The odds are in my favor on that one, but the chances of you locating Charlie just dropped to nearly zero."

"Pfft." She bared her teeth in frustration. "They might take you back, but then they'd bury you in a cell, and you'd never see daylight again."

"How touching." His voice dripped sarcasm. "I had no idea you cared. I'm a Nameless One, remember? The bastards who made your life one ongoing hell—"

"Shut the fuck up," she sputtered. "This isn't helping." Hope slowed to a walk. "We need back up." She narrowed her eyes. "Why didn't you or Tony mention a second compound in the Bangor area? Milton and Roy might've deployed us differently if they suspected we were walking into a potential trap."

"I can't speak for Tony—" Frank alluded to his fellow geneticist, who'd defected with him "—but I assumed the CIA operation up here knocked out both compounds. Remember the map Glory projected into the CIA mainframe from her memory banks?"

"Of course." Hope swallowed hard. "How could I forget? The night she stole that geographic data from the compound's mainframe was the same night she rescued all of us from certain death. Hell, she almost died herself when freaks blew up the tunnel."

Frank's harsh expression softened. "If Roy hadn't gone back for her, she would have died. Back to the map she stole, though. It had the locations for every compound. I'd never have agreed to a chopper with only three of us to pick up that Cortexiphan, if I suspected this place was still a hotbed for freaks."

Breath whistled from between her clenched teeth. "I just ran the odds again. They've fallen to under twenty percent—and most of that's on your side. We need to alert Langley."

Or Charlie won't have any chance at all.

Her heart, the heart she wasn't supposed to have in her genetically modified body, ached. Hope gave herself a brisk mental slap. Only thing she'd achieve storming the freaks' compound like a latter-day version of the cavalry would be to get herself imprisoned.

Same as with Frank, they probably wouldn't kill her. She was too useful alive. They'd dump her in with their female pool and put her to work where they required extra hands. And they'd harvest eggs from her ovaries for their test-tube baby projects.

Frank shook his head. "If we activate our communicators or our wrist computers, it's as good as lighting a flare. Freaks will run us to ground."

Hope shuffled scenarios. "Milton or Roy surely know our bird went down by now, which means help is on its way. How far do we have to be from the bloody, fucking compound before activating our wrist computers isn't a risk?"

"Maybe seven miles." He turned a hundred eighty degrees from the way they'd been headed and ran hard, using his enhanced genetics. This time, he sprinted toward the dirt road they'd been paralleling and used its relatively flat surface to run faster.

Hope paced him. It killed her to run away from Charlie rather than toward him, but they were his only hope, and it would take a minimum of twenty-five agents to take out the compound fast enough the freaks wouldn't hang Charlie out to dry as a hostage.

"Nah. Fifty by my guess." Frank shot a meaningful look her way.

"Gawk. Stay out of my head."

"Sorry. Second nature. Why Charlie?" Frank's question came out of the blue.

"It's none of your business, but why not?"

He shrugged. "Charity's happy enough with Tony. Seems to me we should stick with our own kind."

"You're sounding a whole lot like the human equivalent of a racist. Glory's happy with Roy, and Honor is a great partner for Milton. Neither of them worried about crossing genetic lines."

"Like hell, they didn't." Frank's voice was a growl. "I admit I wasn't here, but I can imagine Kincaid went through more than a few mental changes. He'd hunted us for seven years. Granted Glory can be pretty persuasive, but—"

"You are such an egotistical pig." Hope spoke over him. "Roy pursued Glory. She was scared half to death. She'd just killed a Nameless One and was on the run from our compound."

"I don't need a history lesson. My point was—"

"I got your point, and I disagree." Hope drew to a halt. "We've covered five miles, and we were a couple from the compound. I say we're far enough to risk using our wrist computers."

Before Frank could protest, she bent over hers, clicking keys. A delighted whoop escaped before she could pull it back.

"What?" Frank dragged her wrist to eye level, so he could read the display.

Hope yanked her wrist back, tapping the display a few more times. "Charlie's safe." A broad smile split her face. "Oh yeah, Langley's sending a bird to pick us up at coordinates about five point three miles north northwest of here."

"How'd he escape?" Frank demanded, looking as flummoxed as she'd ever seen him. Normally, none of them indulged in emotional displays.

The sound of boots pounding toward them drove her heart into overdrive. Hope spun, hands raised to channel kinetic power. It was quicker and faster than bullets. Though a gun hung from a holster at her waist, she far preferred her native power. The brittle taste of adrenaline flooded her mouth.

"Shit! Guess we weren't far enough from the compound after all," she gritted out, prepared to take a stand where they were.

How many had the compound sent after them? More importantly, how the hell had they caught up so fast? She sent threads from her augmented genetics spinning outward, prepared to follow them with killing energy the moment she landed on a target.

"Hold up!" Frank dove in front of her.

She feinted to the side. "What are you doing? Get out of my way. We need to fight. We need to—"

"It's me," blasted into her head, and she dropped her hands.

Charlie.

Her heart thudded against her ribcage, each beat a painful reminder of how close she'd come to killing him. Breath left her in a rush as Charlie rounded a bend and came into view bolting down the hard-packed dirt road. Hope did deploy her kinetics then, searching for damage to Charlie's body. She and Frank could fix most injuries if need be.

She started toward Charlie, intent on scanning him from all sides, and then forced herself to remain next to Frank. It wasn't as if she were Charlie's wife or even his girlfriend. She was just one more soldier under his command.

No more. No less.

Charlie drew even with them, breathing harder than she would've had she been running next to him. He slugged each of them on the shoulder and beamed. "Excellent. We all got out. Bastards took my wrist computer and my phone. I radioed Langley when I parachuted out of the bird, and I was headed for a rendezvous point when HQ alerted me you two were safe."

"Absent communication devices, how did you connect with Langley?" Frank asked.

"Stopped at a farmhouse and used their landline." Charlie snorted laughter. "I didn't have any ID on me. Freaks took it along with my electronics. The old man and his wife weren't sure whether they could believe me or not, but the guy finally allowed as to how I could use his phone."

"How'd you break out of the freak compound?" Frank stared hard at Charlie as if assessing whether he were real or some macabre projection.

Hope held back, grateful Frank was peppering Charlie with questions. She felt awkward, and the last thing she wanted was for Charlie to catch a glimpse of her roiling emotions. It was bad enough Frank had guessed about her infatuation. She crossed her fingers and said a silent prayer he'd keep his mouth shut. None of them were long on social skills, so it would be very like Frank to blurt out something that would embarrass the holy shit out of her.

"Let's get moving," Charlie said. "We have a chopper to meet. I'm disappointed we'll be returning without the Cortexiphan, but we'll figure out another angle."

"Probably not," Frank muttered.

"Say more. The CIA isn't into failure." Charlie set a brisk pace.

"Do you actually believe the freaks you just gave the slip to don't know why you showed up here? Even before they shot us down, they collected the drug from the ruins of the other compound and have it well-hidden."

"Tell me again exactly what it's good for," Charlie demanded. "I know it's useful when one of your genomes has a meltdown, like Charity's did. Does it have other uses? When I risk my ass for something, I like to know all about it."

"It maximizes psi potential for everyone—human and our kin alike," Frank replied. "But it has a hell of a side effect punch. Worse for humans, though. Much worse. Statistically, forty-three point six percent of those dosed with it develop a significant delusional disorder. One that's not amenable to treatment with psychiatric drugs. Eight percent die, and an additional seventeen percent become so paranoid they're worthless."

"What are the percentages for us again?" Hope asked.

"It varies." Frank exhaled sharply. "Anywhere from less than three percent to seven."

"But it saved Milton," Charlie cut in.

Breath hissed through Frank's teeth and he made a chopping motion with one hand.

"What?" Charlie demanded. "If it pulled Milton through that tailspin he went into after he had the injection series, that means it has other uses. Right?"

Frank's nostrils flared. "Yes. That's precisely what it means, but I never want to be thrust into the position of experimenting with it under uncontrolled conditions again. Tony and I had no idea what effect it would have piled atop the injections, but Milton was dying and we were fresh out of options."

Charlie shrugged. "Gutsy. You tossed the dice and won. It's the stuff CIA agents are made of. On a more practical note, what that tells me is we need to get our hands on enough Cortexiphan—or get you the shit to synthesize more—so you can run those gold standard, double blind, placebo controlled tests in a nice, cushy lab space."

"When will I ever be out of the field long enough to do that?" Frank demanded. "I'm a scientist, not a soldier. I miss my *nice, cushy lab space.*"

"Good question." Charlie shot a sunny smile his way and turned right at the next intersection.

"You never did tell us how you escaped," Hope spoke up.

"Used kinetics to blow my wrist shackles. Once I was free, I went out a window. Still have a hell of a headache."

"They had you in a shielded room that boomeranged your power right back at you, huh?" Frank asked.

"Yeah. That's my guess. But when I focused my mind ability locally, inside the room, it worked like a champ. Guess the word about the injections hasn't traveled widely."

"Ha! That gig is up now," Frank said sourly. "They'll figure out easily enough how you escaped. Your psi signature will be all over those broken cuffs."

Hope trotted to an empty field and stopped. Shielding her eyes with a hand, she scanned the skies. No chopper, but she hadn't expected to see one since she hadn't heard the characteristic *whump-whump* of rotors.

"Let me see your computer." Frank stepped to her side and grabbed her wrist. "Maybe this isn't the right place."

Hope twisted her face into a scowl and jerked her wrist back. "It is. Give me some credit."

"Oh for Christ's sake, give it a rest you two," Charlie barked. "Hope, he's not a Nameless One anymore. Frank, she's not chattel for you to order about. Got it?" He crossed his arms over his chest and stared both of them down.

"Got it," Frank grunted.

Hope nodded once sharply. Heat rose to her face, and she redirected blood from her capillary beds before she turned bright red. She bent her head and reexamined the coordinates, checking them against the mapping program that lived in her head.

Yup. This was the correct place. Where was the bird? It wasn't like Langley's pilots to be late.

Charlie extended a hand toward her. "Give me your wrist computer." She handed it over and he bent over the device, tapping keys. His forehead creased into a frown. "According to Langley's ATC, the chopper should be here. Guy told me he lost it on radar a few minutes back and thought maybe freaks had sent up some kind of flak."

His hazel eyes developed the glittery, hard edge they always got when danger was imminent. "Drop back," he ordered. "We're exposed as hell here."

Hope held out a hand for her computer, but Charlie shook his head. "I'll hang onto this for now."

She glanced around them. Drop back, where? The sere New England winter countryside barely held bushes. Trees were in short supply, although they'd passed a forest closer to the compound.

"Do you want to retrace our steps?" she asked.

"No." Charlie scanned the wrist computer's display, punching keys with a vengeance. "Follow me. Do what you can to shield your presence."

"Like what?" Frank asked. "Freak energy burns like a fucking beacon—for other freaks. Maybe we should split up. You'd be safer."

Charlie, who'd begun running hard, didn't bother to look back. Or answer.

With a shrug, Frank took off after him. Hope loped behind, her senses on red alert for danger. Freaks didn't maintain a stable of helicopters or planes, but they could pilot anything with an engine by linking to the computers that ran them. It meant they could steal aircraft, defeating their door and ignition locks with their minds.

The thought had no sooner materialized when the thin, high drone of a small, private jet reached her hyper-tuned ears. At first, she cringed, but then she considered what it meant. Planes weren't like choppers. They needed runways to land, so unless the plane was planning to drop a bomb on them, they didn't have much to worry about.

Charlie led them through frozen mud into a stunted, evergreen forest. Snow flurries spit from the gunmetal sky above. Hope's feet were growing numb, and she instructed more blood to warm her toes. Her flight suit was thick and warm, but she snugged its hood more tightly around her head. Days were short this time of year, and the temperature was dropping fast as light leached from the day.

She joined the men where they crouched in the midst of a tight circle of trees. "What about the plane?" She kept her voice low, even though there was no reason to.

"Needs a place to land." Charlie's words mirrored her thoughts.

"Do you think it's freaks?" she persisted.

"That was a stupid question," Frank snapped. "You could've checked easily enough."

Hope bit back annoyance. Frank was just like all the other Nameless Ones. Insufferably arrogant. "Did you?" she shot back.

"Yeah. Now that you mention it, and it's us up there."

"That's an *us* you're no longer part of." Charlie's tone was devoid of inflection—and deadly serious.

Hope was delighted to have Frank put in his place—for once. "What do you suppose—?" she began when an explosion rocked her back on her heels. The sky lit brilliant blue white, and nearby branches cracked as they broke, showering them with bits of wood.

Explains what they can do in a plane they can't land, she thought sourly.

"Fuck!" Charlie pounded a fist into the ground. He didn't have gloves, and his knuckles were raw and red from the cold.

The computer strapped to his wrist flashed with an incoming message. "Double fuck," Charlie muttered. "Bird they sent went down a couple miles from here. At least the pilot punched out."

"Will they send another?" Hope asked.

"Negative. We have to hoof it ten miles to a little town called Smithville."

"What happens there?" Frank asked.

"One of the team should be waiting with a car."

Yeah, right. Maybe.

Hope shut her mind off.

Not all of the CIA were delighted freaks were now part of their ranks. Who knew? Maybe today's sabotage had come from within. It seemed awfully convenient local freaks had known a new chopper was coming for them. Known its location accurately enough to target it and shoot it down. Hell, if she rolled the clock backward, someone had known about *their* bird with enough lead-time to plan its destruction as well.

Taking their chances with the plane, they took off at a hardy lope. She shadowed the men as night grew around them. After dropping the single bomb—and presumably taking out the chopper with focused kinetics—the plane had departed precipitously, almost as if someone were after it. Hope bit her tongue, but something in her energy must have given away her inner turmoil.

"What's up?" Charlie asked, glancing her way.

"I'm worried we have a mole in the operation. We had one before. Remember? The guy in that first batch of recruits."

"I haven't forgotten." Steel sat beneath Charlie's words. "And it's the same conclusion I came to. Need to hit up Milton and Roy as soon as we get back."

The way things were shaping up, Hope wasn't at all certain they'd get back, but she kept that thought buried deep. It wasn't very soldierly, and more than anything, she wanted Charlie to respect her skill and ability. It was where he lived, and the only way she might inveigle herself into his arms.

Shit! I'm pathetic. I'm running for my life. Last thing I should be doing is mooning over some dude who doesn't even know I'm alive.

CHAPTER 3

Charlie blessed the series of half a dozen injections he'd had to make him more like the freaks he'd hunted for the seven years since they'd escaped their handlers and gone rogue. He was beyond tired, but his body still had juice to keep going. Even though it wasn't much past five, it was full dark, and the temperature had dropped to single digits. His feet, encased in heavy winter boots, slipped on ice from time to time.

Would the car and driver actually make it to Smithville?

Good question. Given what had happened with the helicopter, he gave it about fifty-fifty. Hope's theory about an infiltrator in their midst made sense.

Hope.

He cast a surreptitious glance her way, enjoying the effortless flow of her body as she ran. Unlike him, she wasn't breathing hard. Neither was Frank, but when he assessed the other man, lines of strain carved into his face.

Charlie moved closer to him. "Is anything wrong?"

Frank skinned his teeth back from his lips. "Nothing much. Freaks are trying to batter their way inside my head."

The implications of that hit home. "Which means they know precisely where we are," Charlie muttered.

"No. Not unless they break through my defenses." Frank shook his head, hard. "I wish they'd find some other patsy to harass. I'm having to focus a piss pot of kinetics to keep them at bay."

"Would it be easier if we went slower?" Charlie asked.

"No. I should separate from you two, though. That way, I can let them find me, and it would only be me."

Grudging admiration for Frank filled him, but Charlie snapped, "Request denied. We're staying together. I won't let you set yourself up as a decoy. They'd capture you."

"Yeah, but that would give you and Hope a chance to make it back to Langley. I know how they think. If they get me, they'll let this drop."

"Nah, they'll just switch to me," Hope spoke up. "I know how they think too, and they're running scared."

"Not that scared," Frank said. "When we panic, we go to ground, just like we did those first few years after we blew up the compounds and ran. Arrgh. Hurts." He squeezed his eyes shut for a moment.

"Is there anything Hope and I can do to shield you?" Charlie asked. "We're still about four miles from Smithville. Half an hour by my estimate."

"Four point six," Frank gritted out, "but the time estimate is accurate."

Snow, which had begun earlier, fell harder, turning the world around them white. Charlie bent over the wrist device and brought up a map with its GPS function. A few more clicks brought good news.

"We're changing course," he told Frank and Hope. "Follow me."

"Why?" Frank's voice sounded tense and edgy. "This will be easier once I don't have to run and keep the fuckers on the far side of my shielding."

Charlie resisted an urge to tell Frank to go to hell. None of the freaks working for the CIA had squat in the way of military training, and it made running teams with them difficult. "I'm your commanding officer. Trust my orders."

"Goes against the grain," Frank muttered.

Charlie ran faster. Thank Christ Hope wasn't giving him any shit. He slithered down an ice-slick bank and crossed a frozen river, slipping and sliding on its glassy surface. The steep bank on the far side was studded with ice-coated rocks. He dialed in his augmented vision and found what he sought. An opening in the cliff face was just above. It wasn't much of an opening. If he hadn't seen it on the map, he'd never have known it was here.

"Brilliant," Frank said. "I figured out where we were headed crossing the river."

"Someone want to fill me in?" Hope asked.

Instead of answering, Charlie twisted sideways to enter the remains of a lead mine left over from the middle of the nineteenth century. He could see, but he pulled a penlight from his service belt anyway, shining it around a circular chamber roughly twenty feet across.

Frank sank to his haunches at the far side of the chamber. "Thank fucking Christ. The kinetic torture stopped." He glanced around. "Lead mine, huh? That's what's shielding me."

"Correct," Charlie replied. "We're going to stay here for a while. Long enough for your erstwhile kin to think they lost you and look elsewhere."

"Lead." Hope craned her neck as she took in the chamber. "Either it's shielding us from freak kinetics, or it's spreading them so they can't find us."

"It's functioning the same way our shielded rooms do," Frank cut in. "Bouncing their seeking energy right back at them. Hope it hurts like hell."

Charlie started to chide Frank on his continuing use of *us* and *our*, but he'd sounded positively delighted about dishing out pain to the freaks, so Charlie let it drop.

"What about the car?" Hope asked. "Won't they worry if they get there and can't find us?"

"Nothing I can do about that right now," Charlie said. "I'd have to go outside to transmit, and if I activate my communicator to send anything, the freaks will home in on it."

He perched on a large, flat rock at one end of the cavern. "We're here for at least the next hour, so do what you can to get comfy."

Breath whooshed from Frank, and he rubbed his temples. "I didn't appreciate how much energy it took to keep those fuckers at bay until I could stop." He eyed Charlie. "Thank you."

"No need." Charlie kept his voice gruff. "I know your group is shy on military protocol training, but when your field commander gives an order, you follow it without question."

"Kind of like how you Nameless Ones treated the women," Hope piped up, looking pleased with herself.

The corners of Charlie's mouth twitched, but he stifled the smile that wanted out. The women had drawn a raw deal in the freak compounds. They were far stronger than the men, a niggling little secret the men tried their damnedest to hide.

"Stuff it." Frank cast a withering glance her way.

"So long as we went to ground, let's use the time well." Charlie looked from Frank to Hope. "Lend your computer-esque brains to help me think through who might've infiltrated our group at Langley. I figure it's one of the new freaks who took Milton up on his amnesty offer after our mission in the swamp."

"Not necessarily." Hope looked away.

Charlie waited, but she didn't offer anything further. "You have to say more than that," he urged.

She hadn't sat down, and she walked to him and stood, arms crossed beneath her breasts, her breath steaming white in the chill air of the cave. "Remember how you felt about us at first?"

"Yeah. Of course. I was part of the CIA's Black Ops unit assigned to hunt renegade freaks." Charlie smiled crookedly. "That was before I got to know you."

"Exactly," Hope ground out. "We—" she jerked her chin Frank's way "—were the enemy. You didn't like us. Didn't trust us. Wanted to wipe us off the face of the earth. Lots of folk at Langley still feel that way."

"It's true," Frank broke in. "I sense it everywhere at Langley." He hesitated. "It's subtle, but sometimes people leave an area I've entered. Not immediately. They're discreet about it."

"Or they move to the far side of the gym or to another cafeteria table," Hope said. "From what I've observed, lots of the agents don't believe we belong at Langley. Like it's some kind of sacred soil, and we're interlopers."

"Well said." Frank nodded approval.

"Thanks. Coming from you, that's high praise."

Charlie frowned. He'd known there was some backlash at the front end when Glory and four other women had joined them, but he'd assumed it had died down. "Is what you described universal?"

"What do you mean?" Hope asked.

"Have the other freaks, er, genetically modified humans, living at Langley had the same experience? Where you feel you're on the receiving end of bigotry?"

"How could we not?" Frank spoke up. "You call us freaks. Because it was easier and shorter than 'genetically modified humans,' we picked up the banner, and now we call ourselves that. When we tried to come up with a different name, it never stuck."

Charlie refocused on what lay beneath Hope's words. "You're suggesting it doesn't have to be one of you instigating sabotage."

"That's exactly what I'm saying," she replied and held up one hand, counting off on her fingers. "It's not any of us five women. Certainly not Frank or Tony. Or the other small group that came in when Milton offered amnesty. That leaves the ones we picked up in the swamp. You'll recall a couple of them ended up dead rather than defect."

"So you believe the group requesting amnesty wouldn't

jeopardize their tenuous standing at Langley." Charlie quirked a brow.

"The odds are less than nine point three percent." Hope continued to stare at him, her green gaze unsettling.

"Did you run the percentages on the mole being someone other than a freak?" Charlie winced. "Damn. We need different jargon."

"Yeah," Frank said. "I just did, and it's fifty-nine point seven percent."

"If we have nine percent here—" Charlie gestured at Hope "—and sixty percent there, it only adds to seventy. What happened to the other thirty?"

"It's an unknown," Hope said. "That's how odds work. When we calculate them, they rarely add to a hundred."

Charlie eyed the wrist computer he'd commandeered from Hope. Forty minutes had passed. Was it enough time? The thought of sabotage going on under their noses at Langley was deeply disturbing. When they'd identified the first mole, it was a freak specifically sent to infiltrate their operation. Glory had figured it out, and Roy had killed him.

It bothered him far more that today's problems might have their roots in an agent feeding information to the freaks who'd taken out their small chopper—and the one sent to pick them up.

"Talk to us." Hope still stood over him. "Help us understand how you think."

Charlie got to his feet so he could look across at Hope, rather than up at her. Even though she looked human, and had a lot of human traits, she'd spent her entire life on a different path. One that didn't include indoctrination into the culture he took for granted.

"Prejudice runs deep," he began.

"I get that." She spun one hand in a come along gesture. "We hated the Nameless Ones, but we hated you worse. And we were scared of normal humans."

"Maybe not so much scared," Frank cut in, "but we viewed you as inferior. Arbitrary and capricious, but stupid." He stood too and walked over to join them. "Seven years after we exited stage left, you were still hunting for us." He shrugged. "You were damned easy to fool, all in all."

Defensiveness rose, hot and brittle. Charlie choked back a stream of excuses. They had no place here. He directed his energy on the problem at hand and said, "Maybe at first, when it was just the five women at Langley, most people looked the other way."

Hope nodded. "Yeah. After all, no one pays much attention to us. One of the parts that's the same for freaks and normal humans is women are relegated to inconsequential status."

"I don't feel that way." Charlie kicked himself. His personal beliefs and attitudes had no place in a conversation with his subordinates.

"A lot of your men do," Frank said. "I've overheard them talking." He cocked his head to one side, listening and made a chopping motion with one hand.

"What?" Charlie switched to telepathy.

"Freaks. Found us. I have no fucking idea how."

"I do," Hope said. *"They tracked me. That barrage of kinetics they pummeled Frank with was so much chaff. Shit. I shielded myself, but not well enough."* She squared her shoulders and narrowed her eyes, facing the cave's entrance. "Bring it on, motherfuckers," she growled.

Charlie drew his sidearm. Dropping into a shooter's stance, he trained his weapon at the doorway, listening intently. Moments dripped past, and then he heard boots scraping over the frozen river. How the hell had Frank picked up on them as soon as he did? They must've been on the far side of the river when he'd warned them.

"Weapons," Charlie hissed.

"We'll use kinetics," Frank said. *"No bullets to ricochet."*

It was a good argument, but Charlie's command of kinetics wasn't as solid as his ability to point and shoot a gun. Adrenaline hummed along his nerves. After the day he'd had, it surprised him. He was certain he'd run the well damn near dry.

The scrabbling of hands and boots on ice-slick rock grew louder. How many were there? He flicked off the safety on his .45 semiautomatic and located a spare clip.

"Listen to me. Shoot to kill. The second you see a freak, blast them. This is a defensible position because the entrance is so narrow, only one at a time can get through."

"Don't bother with telepathy, human," a harsh male voice shouted from outside. "You never learned to shield your communication, so save your primitive kinetics."

"What the fuck do you want with us?" Frank yelled.

"Since you asked," the voice went on, "a number of things. You for one. We're short of geneticists, and V4 has instabilities that are worse than V3."

"Ha!" Frank exhaled sharply. "I figured as much. The thing with V3 is at least I understood how to fix us."

"One more reason we need you back," a second voice said. "Full amnesty and privileges reinstated immediately."

Charlie skewered Frank with his gaze, not liking how this was going. "Well?"

Frank shook his head. "You said *a number of things*." He projected his voice toward the cave's entrance. "What are the others?"

"Of course we'll want the woman. If nothing else, we can harvest eggs from her ovaries." The second voice had all the inflection of a man reading off a grocery list.

"Not going to happen," Charlie said through clenched teeth.

"That's her decision, human," the first voice retorted. "Not yours."

"Why in the hell would I want to return?" Hope's voice shook a little. "I had nothing in my compound. Not even enough blankets to be warm at night. Skimpy, rationed food—"

"Enough!" the second voice boomed. "We all lived on short rations."

"Not in my compound," Hope countered. "The Nameless Ones ate damn well. It was only the women who got shortchanged—for everything." She took a ragged breath. "I'll die before I return to a compound."

"It might come to that, bitch," voice number one said.

"Several is more than two," Frank broke in. "What else do you have in mind?"

"The human, the one with delusions of competence, has apparently gotten some chemical assistance to make him more like us. We plan to take him alive to study just how his composition differs. He might yield clues to evening out V4."

The freak's jibe about delusions of competence rankled. Charlie ignored it. Losing his temper wasn't wise. He'd been hotheaded as a youth, and spent more time regretting rash actions than congratulating himself on muscling through dicey situations.

He kept his gun trained on the entrance and edged toward it, intent on maybe getting a shot off—if he could get the angle right.

"So." He kept the word light, conversational. "What makes you think all three of us are going to waltz out of here and turn ourselves over to you?"

"We have dynamite," a different voice chimed in. "If you refuse, we'll leave a bunch of sticks just at the cave's opening and light a long fuse. The ceiling will cave in. Even if you survive the blast, the three of you will never be able to dig your way out."

A muted *thunk* sounded like a cannon blast as a bundle of dynamite sticks materialized just inside the cave.

Charlie scooted forward, hauled a booted foot back and kicked the roll of sticks back outside. "Primitive," he scoffed. "You'd be better off with grenades."

Frank motioned Charlie back across the cave. He'd typed something on the screen of his communicator. Charlie leaned close and read.

Cave must have a back entrance. All of them do.

Hope scuttled close enough to read it. Giving a thumbs-up sign, she took off running through the rounded opening at the far end of the cave.

Another *thunk* and more dynamite—or maybe it was the same bundle—landed a bit farther inside.

"I've got this," Frank muttered. With his augmented physical ability, he crossed the cave, punted the explosive so hard Charlie saw sparks, and was back next to Charlie in seconds.

A sharp boom rocked the ground beneath their feet. Charlie's ears rang as sound waves reverberated. He wanted to clap his hands over them, but then he'd have to let go of his weapon, and he wasn't about to do that.

"What the hell?" Charlie shook a fist at the door. "Damn shit isn't supposed to detonate without a blasting cap."

"We can ignite it with kinetics," Frank gritted. "The good news is it was supposed to blow in here, not out there. Even better news is that I was fast enough to defeat them."

Charlie winced. If it had been him, the shit would've blown up about the time he reached it. Contemplating his own mortality never held any allure, so he asked, "Wonder if any of them are left?"

"Only one way to find out. But we can afford to wait until we can hear again. My ears are in worse shape than yours right now, but they'll recover faster."

A long, low whistle cut through the ringing in Charlie's ears.

Frank grabbed his arm and pulled, gesturing the way Hope had run. Charlie opened his mouth to ask if Frank thought she'd found a way out, but the other man shook his head.

"Yeah, right," Charlie mumbled. "Not thinking." He spun in a one-eighty and trotted after Frank's disappearing form.

The freak followed a downward-sloping track littered with large rocks. Charlie's night vision was better than a normal human's, but after the second time he caught a boot tip on rocks he hadn't seen, he pulled out his penlight and balanced his gun atop it. He wanted to ask Frank how he knew where he was going, but maybe this was a time to trust that one freak could pinpoint another. It was how the explosive-happy group had located them.

He'd thought the lead in the mine would conceal them, but it hadn't. All it did was stop the constant barrage on Frank's shielding.

They splashed through standing water as they wended lower, farther into the mountainside by Charlie's navigational deductions. His computer was worthless down here.

A second blast rumbled behind him. Charlie didn't have to guess what it was. Apparently, enough freaks had survived the first explosion to toss more dynamite into the cave and detonate it.

No going back. He stuffed his gun into its holster. He might need it later, but not right now. He caught up with Frank and asked, "Where is she?"

"There should be a side tunnel leading upward in about a hundred more feet."

"Which side?" Charlie asked.

"Right. There it is." Frank pointed. "Hope's at the top looking outside."

"Can she see the fuckers who blew up our cave?"

"Don't know. You can ask her soon enough." Frank slowed and turned to face Charlie. "She cares about you, but don't let her know I told you. She'd be furious."

Charlie rocked back on the balls of his feet as if he'd been slapped. "But that's impossible. She's— No, I'm— Aw, fuck. Never mind."

"Ssht," Frank hissed. "Probably should've kept my mouth closed."

Charlie didn't need a second invitation to shut up. Like he always did when things threatened to become personal, he buried what Frank just said deep. Their only goal was survival, and it wasn't at all certain they'd get back to Langley in one piece.

He rounded a ninety-degree curve and saw Hope standing at the top of a steep trail, her silhouette outlined by the night sky. Her hood still covered her head, but tendrils of black hair had escaped, framing her face. They gave her a vulnerable look that tugged at his heart.

Frank reached her first and looked outside. "Jesus, Hope," he sputtered. "I thought you said this was a way out."

"It is," she shot back. "We'll just have to climb a little. You're one ungrateful son of a bitch. I found the only other way out of here and—"

"Enough." Charlie reached them sucking air and wishing he was as strong as the freaks. He glanced out the opening. Precipitous rock fell away. The two hundred feet directly below them were extremely difficult before the angle eased off.

"We can't go back," he said. "So it's this or nothing."

"Yeah, I know," Frank replied. "That last explosion sealed the entrance." He screwed his face into a mask of concentration and stared at the sheer rock face. "This side—" he pointed "—is a better bet. With zero climbing experience but our superior coordination, we have a sixty-seven percent chance of surviving."

Charlie, whose climbing forays had mostly been in gyms with ropes under more or less controlled conditions, didn't bother asking what his odds were. They needed ropes, hardware, climbing shoes with sticky soles. Absent those, navigating the sheer granite face would be damned difficult.

"I have a better idea," Charlie said and keyed his wrist computer. Once he got Langley, he bent over the device, keeping his voice so low he couldn't hear himself with his damaged ears. If he couldn't hear, neither could the freaks—if any were still milling around below. He doubted it. They'd assume their job was done and scuttle out of there like the insects they were.

"McClaren. Spit it out." the tinny voice interrupted his musings.

He rattled off their coordinates, then requested a chopper. It could drop harnesses and ropes to get them into the bird. Once he was done, he hunkered with his back against a wall and patted the rocky ground. "May as well take a load off," he said. "We'll be here for a while."

Frank cocked his head to one side. "My ears are mostly clear again. Cars leaving. Three, no make that four."

"Are you certain it's freaks?" Charlie asked.

"Of course I'm certain." Frank rolled his amber eyes. "I sense them the same way they tracked us. They figure we're goners, so they're on their way back to the compound."

"How long will we be here?" Hope asked, following it with, "What makes you think this bird will get through?"

Charlie met her clear, green eyes and shrugged. "I don't know. Third time's a charm, maybe."

Frank's words from earlier slammed into his guts, but he pushed the information aside. Even if Hope were interested in him, he'd sworn off woman for a host of good reasons, and none of them had changed.

CHAPTER 4

*H*ope paced back and forth. Adrenaline still hummed along her nerves, and she was too keyed up to sit. The opening high on the cliff face made no sense. Why create it if it was a dead end? Her brain functioned like a computer with infinite storage. She'd downloaded reams of data into it, much of which she'd never examined. Since she had time, she riffled through her memory banks for everything she could come up with about mines in the eastern United States a hundred years ago.

Back at her compound, she'd worked with their mainframe and purloined information out of it whenever she could, figuring the stray bits of data might come in useful sometime. In those days, she'd plotted to find a way out of the compound and out from beneath the Nameless Ones' control. Today held a few similarities because she was trapped and hunting for solutions.

"There's got to be another path out of here," she muttered.

"Why?" Charlie asked. "It's little shy of a miracle you located this egress point."

Hope licked dry lips. The chapped places hurt, and she focused her body's energy to heal them. "Because when I looked up mines—"

"Looked them up where?" he interrupted.

"In my head, where else?" Hope sounded like a shrew, but it didn't matter. Charlie was nothing but a pipe dream. Just because Glory and Honor had hooked up with normal humans, maybe Frank was onto something when he'd said they should stick with their own kind.

"Go ahead." Charlie focused his gaze on her. He didn't apologize for interrupting, but he didn't have to. He ran things here, and she'd do well to keep that front and center.

"Old mines, ones like this that are left over from the eighteen hundreds, almost always had escape hatches. This place we're standing was likely an extra way of shunting oxygen into the mine in case of a cave in. Or if the mining chemicals poisoned the air."

"You told me this was the only other way out," Frank said.

"Yeah. I know, but maybe I was wrong." Hope turned on her heel and trotted back down the steep track that led to the main passageway through the mine.

"Where are you going?" Charlie called after her.

"To hunt for another way out of here. We have at least an hour, maybe two. I'll be back soon enough."

Hope kept moving, afraid Charlie would order her to return if she stayed put. Schematics for lots of mines resided in her memory, but not this one. She entered the main tunnel again and sent her kinetics spinning outward, seeking variances in the damp walls rising around her. Nothing promising pinged back, so she walked deeper into the cave system. This may have been an active lead mine, but the cave system was natural. Miners had taken advantage of it to avoid the work of excavating tunnels.

At least it was warmer than it had been looking out at falling snow on the windy precipice. Hope passed numerous side passages, but they all angled down. That may have worked to reach veins of ore, but they'd just lead her deeper into the mountain. She needed a way out—not farther in. Catching her bearings, she hurried forward. The end of the cave system was close. She felt a change in the way energy bounced back at her. If she didn't find what she sought soon, she'd have to declare defeat and return to the men.

Just because most quarries of this vintage were built with back doors was no reason to assume this mine had one. She could've stuck with Charlie and Frank, but it felt better to be doing something. She hadn't been designed to sit for long periods. In the compounds, physical exercise ate up big chunks of each day. At Langley, she had the gym. And a huge campus where she ran hard every single day to burn off the confusion created by living and interacting with normal humans.

I'm making excuses.

I was afraid if I spent too much time with Charlie, he'd figure out how much I like him.

She reached the end of the natural cave system. Someone had drilled a narrow tunnel in the end of it, but she'd have had to crawl through the thing. When she bent and shot kinetic energy past the opening, it bounced back at her.

That settled it. The tunnel extension was jammed with debris. She'd never get through.

Hope focused her augmented vision and scanned the walls, paying attention to every nuance. She hadn't found any side corridors leading upward, which meant maybe she was looking for the wrong thing.

Nothing jumped out at her, so she moved to the side of the cavern, determined to examine it carefully before she gave up. She'd almost passed a jumble of rocks when steps carved into limestone drew her attention. Breath caught in her throat. This must be it. Why built a series of risers on the outside wall if it wasn't a way out? All the other mining activity had been on the other side of the cave system.

Hope set her mouth in a tight line. She'd been so focused on finding a passageway, she'd come within an angstrom of totally missing the primitive staircase. Subtle and shallow, it had crumbled to nothing in multiple places, but someone had gone to the trouble to build the damn thing, so it must lead somewhere.

She trotted next to it and placed a foot on the first riser. Rotten stone crumbled beneath her boot the moment she weighted it. The second step wasn't any better. Hope stood beside the rough-hewn stairs, stretched her arms over her head, and reached her fingertips as far possible, curling them around the highest step she could reach.

Hoping like hell the rot was limited to the bottom—because maybe that segment of the stairway had spent time under water—she pulled herself up until she crouched on a step that mercifully held her. Hope waited, but nothing cracked beneath her weight, so she stood and worked her way upward. She did a quick calculation and determined she'd dropped close to a thousand feet since leaving the men. She might not have to regain quite that much elevation, but she'd have to follow the stairs for several hundred feet.

Many steps were missing, and a few disintegrated beneath her, but she was quick and nimble. The stairs hugged the cavern wall, steepening as she climbed higher. A quick glance at lots of empty air off to her right convinced her she needed to make this work. A fall might not kill her, but she'd break something, and extricating her would create problems for everyone.

She'd never wanted to be a bother or a burden. And the last thing she needed was for Charlie to view her as a loose cannon who needed babysitting because she couldn't take care of herself. She'd chosen this project, and she'd see it through to its end.

Hope stopped thinking. She narrowed her focus to the steps beneath her boots. Never mind they were endless. Never mind there might not be a top. Never mind she might come to a place so dicey, even she couldn't navigate it. Her feet had slipped once on a patch of loose rubble, and she'd slithered twenty feet down before she'd latched onto a protruding rock that held.

She'd been far more careful the second time she passed that section, testing each step before she committed her full weight to it.

Anxiety soured her stomach. If this didn't work, getting back down this twisting, winding hodgepodge of uneven steps would take a long time.

A low, guttural growl stopped her dead and made the small hairs on the back of her neck vibrate. The noise came again, reverberating in the pit of her stomach. Her palms slicked with sweat. What the hell was it? The thing sounded big, but something much bigger than her couldn't have managed this stairway.

Not true, the machine part of her brain piped up.

Animals have claws. Four legs would be superior to two for negotiating—

Hope told her inner maven to stand down. She didn't need a comparative zoology lesson. She sent tendrils of kinetic energy upward, seeking the source of the growl.

It had to be an animal, which meant she could kill it, but she hated to. This was its turf. She was the intruder. Would there be a way to reach into its mind and calm it?

Getting ahead of myself. I need to figure out what it is, first.

Mammalian vibrations reached her. It narrowed things down, but not by much. What the hell had she expected? A dinosaur? She cloaked her presence, much as she'd done when they were on the run earlier, and crossed her fingers the creature wouldn't be as savvy as the Nameless Ones pursuing them had been. She slowed her pace and willed herself to move silently. Before, she'd dislodged rocks every other step.

Hope focused every shred of concentration on becoming one with her environment. Her movements became slow, deliberate. It seemed to placate whatever lay in wait because after one more, long, threatening snarl, silence reigned.

The stairs, which had taken a straight line upward, developed a series of switchback turns. She could see why. Whenever they ran up against an outcrop or other obstacle, they doubled back the other way. Her nostrils flared. The scents of raw meat, snow, and fur reached her.

Crap.

She'd been concentrating so hard on negotiating the stairs, she'd let her shielding slip. If she could smell what was above her, it could smell her as well. Another rumble confirmed her fears.

Hope swallowed hard. Her heart hammered against her chest. Would the animal rush her? Drive her from her precarious stance? She shuffled through her mind for information about predators. They respected what stood up to them. She'd do well not to act like prey.

Besides, not much of anywhere to run. Even if she turned back, her downward travels wouldn't be much faster than she was moving right now.

She wished she knew more. Like how far away was the thing? What was it? Bear? Wolf? Mountain lion? Or something smaller and more manageable like a coyote? Was it waiting at the top of the stairs? Did it have a den hogged out of the side of the mountain?

Hope forced herself to use her augmented mind and ruled out bears. They'd be hibernating. Mountain lions weren't native to New England, but bobcats and lynxes were. Wolves had been driven out of Maine decades ago by a combination of hunters and disease.

A thought struck her and she halted, dialing in her sensitive hearing that had recovered from the earlier blast. Muted whines and yips reached her. They explained a lot. Whatever was up there had pups or kits.

It made things easier—and harder. She'd have to be careful. If she killed the mother, its babies would probably die too. It seemed late in the year to be raising a litter of anything, but nature was out of whack, just like everything else in an upside down world where a few freaks had joined their destiny with normal humans.

Noise from below dragged her attention the other way. Were there more of the growling things? Hope sent energy downward and smothered a snort. Frank and Charlie. Apparently, the men couldn't stand her being gone so long.

"Take it easy," she projected.

"Why?" Frank retorted. *"I feel you up there."*

"Can't be much worse where you are than the bottom of this fucker was," Charlie added.

The animal snarled again. Louder, longer, more serious. Hope silently offered it points for sparing her a blundering explanation.

"Don't move!" Charlie's mind voice blasted her. *"That's an order."*

"What is it?" she asked.

"Lynx. Used to hunt them. Probably a female with kits."

She heard the snick of his weapon as he drew it from its holster.

"Charlie. You can't kill her. The babies will die too."

"Stand down, both of you. I've got this," Frank said.

Hope didn't feel like standing down. "What are you going to do?" she asked out loud. The lynx was aware of them, so they didn't need to bother with telepathy.

"Same thing I did in the swamp with the alligators and snakes. Got lots of practice with how non-human species react." Frank reached her and pressed her against the wall as he worked around her.

Charlie came into view from below, his .45 gripped in one hand.

"Both of you stay put," Frank called back. "I'll let you know when I have this buttoned up."

The lynx screeched outrage.

Hope balled her hands into fists and reached outward with kinetics. What had worked for reptiles might not be as effective for a pissed off mother lynx. She didn't bother with subtlety. The cat knew they were there. A red ball of fury formed in her mind, followed by a second one, both hurtling toward them.

"Frank," she screamed. "There are two."

"You think I don't— Ooph." A blast of white heat from Frank lit up the cavern, and a high, thin shriek filled the air. One of the ruby balls faded, flickering as life drained from it. Rocks cascaded noisily as the lynx fell, but boots scrabbling over rubble suggested Frank had tumbled right along with it.

"Frank. Report," Charlie barked.

"I'm fine. Damn thing must've weighed seventy pounds. Knocked me off the stairs, but I didn't fall far."

"Is your position stable?" Charlie asked.

"Yes."

"Remain there."

For once, Frank didn't argue, which meant the animal attack had spooked him. Anger boiled hot. Goddamned, sanctimonious Nameless Ones always thought they knew best. Frank's hubris had killed one of the cats.

Hope tried harder. She augured power into the other animal's mind, but blending calming suggestions with what must feel like an assault weren't a good mix. The lynx kept coming.

Charlie pushed against her. "Out of the way, Hope. Even I can feel it bearing down on us. I've got this. Frank's out of range of my weapon."

She stood firm. "No. I haven't given up yet. Her babies will die."

"They're animals," Charlie insisted. "Move out of my way."

"It's the same thing you used to call us." Bitterness flooded her mouth with a metallic burn. "You can court-martial me for disobedience later, but I'm not done trying to reason with the cat."

Charlie didn't argue. Maybe her point about normal humans seeing those like her as nothing better than animals had gotten through.

She streamed pale, blue light into the cat's mind. Told it they didn't mean it any harm, that they'd walk right by the nest. All they wanted was out of the cavern.

Rather than receding, the cat's temper escalated until the only thing in Hope's mind was pulsating fury. Maybe her message would've gone down easier if Frank hadn't killed the lynx's mate. Claws scraping over dirt grew louder. She had one more chance to get this right.

"Please," she pleaded with the lynx. *"I'm sorry about your mate. We didn't mean—"*

A furred body hurtled from above, dropping onto her back. Claws dug deep, and jaws closed around the back of her neck.

"Goddammit!" Charlie yelled, grappling with the cat from behind her, as he punched it. The animal ignored his fists, screeching its outrage.

Hope was out of options, but she was also still mind-linked to the lynx. She threw her kinetics wide-open and sent killing energy into the creature, feeling like the worst kind of traitor.

Its hold on her loosened as life drained from it. Charlie heaved its body into the abyss next to them. The chasm had been her constant companion all the way up the staircase, and Hope stared down it, wishing there'd been a different outcome. With the lynx dispatched, Charlie wrapped his arms around her from behind, holding her against his chest.

"Hope. Jesus, Hope. Talk to me. I couldn't use my gun. Too close quarters."

It felt good in Charlie's arms. So good, she was tempted to fake a faint, but then she got hold of herself. "I'm okay," she said.

"Thank fucking God." His grip on her didn't loosen.

"Hate to interrupt such a tender moment, but request permission to crawl back up to the stairs." Frank's voice dripped sarcasm. "I understand you wanted to keep me out of range of stray bullets, but that's no longer a danger."

"Come on back here," Charlie called. "Can you help Hope?"

"I don't need his help." She wriggled in Charlie's arms. "What I do need is water so one of you can clean debris out the claw marks."

Charlie let go and focused his light on her back and neck. "Damn good thing we got it in time. It was ready to snap your neck. You've got a couple of fang puncture wounds, but they're not deep. And they didn't cut through anything critical. Your flight suit is thick. It deflected the worst of the damage from the lynx's claws, but some gashes penetrated your skin."

Hope gritted her teeth together and twisted so she faced Charlie. "I know all that. And it wasn't *we* who got it. It was me. I killed it, and I feel really shitty about how this ended." She shook her head hard, but the crushing sense of failure remained. If it had just been her, if the men hadn't shown up, she probably could've dealt with the lynxes without resorting to killing them.

"We need to find the babies. Maybe there's a wildlife rescue in the area. Maybe…" She ran out of words.

Frank bounced onto the stairs a few feet ahead of her. "Let's see what we find in the nest," he said.

"Then we can figure out what to do with them," Charlie added. "Depends how old they are. My guess is they were born last spring, and they're plenty able to provide for themselves."

Hope turned to follow Frank. Her back burned like fury, and her neck was stiff and sore. She funneled healing energy into the claw marks with instructions to destroy any disease-carrying microbes. As she trudged uphill, the memory of how safe she'd felt cradled against Charlie's body filled her mind. She tried to delete that particular memory engram, but it refused to leave.

Or maybe she wasn't trying all that hard.

Another quarter mile, and a chill breeze reached them. Meant her journey up the endless stairs was almost done. They'd been in somewhat better shape at the upper end, but she offered kudos for courage to the miners who'd trotted up and down this aerial expanse, maybe every day.

One more sharp switchback, and she joined Frank, who stood beneath a rounded stone arch leading to a rough track trailing down the mountainside. They were well below the precipitous cliffs that had stymied them above.

"Did you find the babies?" she asked Frank.

He nodded and jerked his chin to the right. "They're in a burrow about ten feet up, but they're not babies. Charlie's guess was right on. They're several months old."

Charlie caught up to them. "So long as they're not nursing, they'll survive. Cats pack up in family groups, kind of like wolves."

"If they're older, why haven't they challenged us?" Hope glanced upward. Extending energy to search for the young lynxes, she identified three.

"They don't know their parents are dead," Charlie said. "Their job is to lay low and let the older ones take care of threats."

"How come you know so much about cat behavior?" Hope asked.

"Follow me down, and I'll tell you. There's a creek at the bottom. It's probably frozen, but we can chop through the ice for water to clean your wounds while we're waiting for the chopper. I'll break out the first aid kit there too and at least get disinfectant on them."

"Want me to check in with Langley on the chopper?" Frank asked, his voice brusque.

"Sure. You might give them our altered coordinates while you're at it. Tell them we'll locate a landing pad at the bottom if we can."

With a last, lingering glance at where the three newly orphaned lynxes had hidden themselves, Hope started down a primitive trail hogged into the side of the mountain. It wasn't in any better shape than the stairs had been, but for something over a century old, it had held up well.

Between pain, her confused feelings for the man behind her, and kicking herself for how clumsily she and Frank had dealt with the lynxes, Hope retreated to her machine side. It almost made it possible not to care what happened next.

Almost, but not quite.

If she could, she'd have lain down and let sleep blot everything out, but sleep and Langley were a long way off.

CHAPTER 5

Charlie trudged behind Hope. He'd almost had a heart attack when the lynx dropped from a hidden ledge far above them right onto her back. He'd angled his pistol and come close to taking a shot, except he might have killed Hope right along with the lynx. If he'd had a smaller caliber weapon, he'd have used it, but the .45 dealt wide-angle destruction, and he couldn't risk it.

Despite his reluctance to admit feeling anything for anyone, even he couldn't ignore that he'd been so relieved she was alive, he'd held her against him. Cradled her and hadn't let go after she'd reassured him she was all right. The scents of honeysuckle, orange, and cinnamon still lingered, tickling his nostrils. Remembering the feel of her pressed against him shot his cock to attention. The curves of her high, tight butt had been snugged against him then, along with her long, sinuous back and broad, well-muscled shoulders. Where he'd reached around her, breasts had pushed against the sides of his arms.

Stop! I have to stop this.

She works for me.

He rolled his mental eyes. The only reason he'd ended up in command of his own unit was because Roy Kincaid had hooked up with Glory. To avoid nepotism, the CIA had shifted the women to Charlie, making him a crew chief. Some days, he missed working for Roy, missed his old team. They'd been a lean, mean bunch of badass hombres.

He snickered at the thought.

"What's so funny? I could use a joke." Hope didn't turn around.

Charlie couldn't answer her, so he asked a question of his own. "You still feeling bad about the lynxes?"

Half-turning, she shot him a pointed look over one shoulder. "Of course I am. If the two of you hadn't come after me— Never mind."

"You were gone for more than an hour," Charlie said. "Frank felt you turn back toward us, but instead of returning, you started to climb. That was when we figured you'd found an alternative way out and followed you. Assuming the next bird makes it to us, we could've let it winch us up with ropes and harnesses, but that would take time with three people. Time we'd be hellishly exposed—if the freaks who blew up the front entrance to the cave left a sentry to report in. And that type of rescue effort assumes the wind doesn't kick up."

"Not that," she said, still sounding despondent. "I wasn't questioning why you caught up with me."

"What then?" Charlie trotted closer so they could talk more easily. It wasn't the best idea, given his attraction, but he did it anyway.

"If I'd been alone, maybe I could've reasoned with the cats. And they'd still be alive. I know you and Frank believe the young ones will be fine, but we murdered their parents. All they were doing was defending their young."

Something wistful and melancholy rode beneath her words. He wanted to draw her against him and stroke hair back from her face. Charlie clasped his hands behind him to avoid the temptation to touch her.

"Everything should work out for the young lynxes. They have good survival skills." His tone was gruffer than he meant it to be.

Before he could apologize, she murmured, "I hope so. I lost over half my family the night Glory sprang us from the compound." Hope shook her head sadly. "Glory offered all twelve of the women in our pod a chance. Seven of us had been so brainwashed by the Nameless Ones, they thought it was a trap and refused. They made a bad decision, one that spelled their deaths."

Hope stopped walking and spun so abruptly he slipped sideways to avoid running into her. Her features were twisted in anguish. "I don't let myself think about that night much. You wouldn't understand, but those women were the sisters I never had. Hell, you were raised in a family. With a mother and father and two brothers. Even before freaks busted out of their original compounds and went on the run, we were born in incubators. I have no fucking idea who my parents were."

He opened his mouth, but she waved him to silence. "I have my parents' names. I rifled through those databanks Glory stole, but they're just names. Parents take care of you. Like those lynxes tried to protect their young. All mine did was donate genetic material."

Hope turned away and ran hard down the trail, skidding on loose rocks.

"Wait." Charlie bolted after her. "I'm sorry the lynxes are dead, but we had no choice. That one on your back would've killed you. Same for the one that attacked Frank. Reason I understand them so well is because I grew up hunting in New England's woods. Once you cornered one, it was you or them. Never any middle ground."

"Knowing I killed it to save myself doesn't make it any easier. Guess my lack of a family makes me a sucker for anything orphaned. Except those snakes and alligators in the swamp. I'm sure baby alligators are cute, but the big ones gave me the creeps."

"Baby snakes are lots of things too, but cute isn't on the menu." Charlie smothered a snort. "How did you know I have two brothers? Did you see it in my mind?"

Hope slowed, but didn't turn around. "Oops. Busted. When

Charity was looking for reasons for Honor not to fall for Milton, she might have hacked into the CIA personnel database."

"Might have?" Charlie forced back the laugh that wanted out. The freaks were amazingly resourceful. Much more so than their human counterparts.

"I'll never tell."

"You just did. What else do you know about me?"

"Not much." Hope hesitated. "I'm sorry about your one brother. The one in the institution. I feel for him, maybe because I did time in the compounds. It's kind of the same."

Something lodged in Charlie's throat, and he swallowed around it. He hadn't thought about Richard in years. "Thanks. He's in the best place for him. He never had the skills to survive on his own. Sees things and hears things that aren't there, and he reacts in bad ways."

Charlie tried to stem the flow of words, but once he'd begun, they pushed their way out. "I tried to tell Mom and Dad, but no one listened until Rick blew up a convenience store because he thought aliens there were controlling his thoughts."

"Are your parents still alive?" Hope flashed a glance over one shoulder.

"Very much so. Dad's an aeronautical engineer, just like me. He's still working. Mom's a nurse. They live a few miles west of the Boston metro area in the same house I grew up in. It's close to the facility where Rick is, and they visit him as much as they can."

Discomfort rocked him, and he tried to dissect it. It wasn't that he'd kept personal details secret. When he'd been in the Seals and then in the CIA, he and his teammates had swapped details about their lives. Was it because Hope was female?

Oh hell no. It's because I care about her. Way too much. And this feels like what couples do when they're getting to know each other.

Too late, he felt the subtle vibration that meant she'd been hovering in his mind. He did catch up with her then and placed his hands gently on her shoulders, careful to avoid the torn places in her flight suit. "Not fair."

"Why?" She angled her head his way. "You can do the same thing —if you choose."

"I found open water," Frank yelled. "Hope, get down here so we can clean those cat scratches."

"Best get moving. We can talk later," Charlie said, recognizing his words as a prime stalling tactic. They could resume their conversation, but he'd see to it they didn't. Not about anything personal at least.

Hope shot a penetrating glance his way before loping down the trail.

Charlie followed at a more sedate pace. It had been easy to talk with Hope. Too easy. She was a good listener and had asked questions that showed she cared. Her insight about his brother had been lined with warmth and understanding, rather than the usual discomfort he sensed whenever someone discovered he had a severely mentally ill sibling.

She hadn't held back about her outrage and distress, but her disclosures about herself made him care even more. He longed to hold her, trace the outline of her full lips with a fingertip and then with his mouth. She might not have grown up in a family, but he could make up for that. He could care for her, make her forget the lonely years when—

Jesus, fucking Christ! Get a grip.

It's not bad enough I want to take her to bed. Now I'm developing a Sir Galahad complex where I want to protect her from everything bad in the world.

Charlie reined in his tumbling emotions, relegating them to a subterranean crawlspace at the bottom of his psyche. Normally, they retreated without much of a fuss. Not tonight. He kicked a rock out of his way and then one more. Used to relying on his wits and his superior physical prowess, he'd be the first to admit he was a total loser when it came to affairs of the heart.

Where the rubber met the tarmac, he had two choices. Slam the door shut on the intimacy that was beginning to develop between him and Hope or have a heart-to-heart with Milton. He couldn't open his heart any farther to Hope and have her in a direct line of command. His feelings would impact his decisions, and it wouldn't be fair to his other subordinates.

Smoke tickled his nostrils, and his eyes widened. Crap! Had Frank lit a fire? That wasn't a good idea. What if the freaks were still milling about? Smoke would give their location away well before the chopper could arrive.

He broke into a run, covering the last half mile to the bottom faster than he imagined he could, given all the shit his body had been through today. Hope crouched at the edge of a streambed near a small fire that someone—either she or Frank—had built between three large rocks. Her flight suit was pushed off her shoulders, and Frank worked over her, sponging water he'd warmed in a battered cookpot over her abraded flesh.

Charlie hurried forward. The sight of Hope's naked shoulders made him want so many things. At the top of the heap, he wanted to be the one touching her. Frank's ministrations felt like a slap in the face.

Focus!

"We can't have a fire," he cried and bent to cup handfuls of snow to douse it.

"Hold up," Frank growled. "Give me a little credit. No freaks anywhere around that I could sense. There are a few farmhouses on the other side of this band of hills. They all have fires going. Even if freaks are shrouding themselves, they'd have a hell of a time sorting our fire from others in this region."

"Good you checked." Charlie kept his tone brusque. Frank's hands on Hope bothered him—but none of it was personal. Personal had no place in the field. "Where'd that pot come from?"

Frank spared him a patronizing glance. "My pack. Any other questions?"

"It's not regulation issue." Charlie felt like an idiot and swallowed the next few words before he made a total ass out of himself.

"Yeah. Lots of my stuff isn't. Want me to empty my rucksack so you can take inventory?"

"Won't be necessary." Charlie tossed the snowballs still clutched in his hands aside.

Hope rotated her shoulder blades. "Feels like there's no more debris," she said.

"There isn't," Frank agreed. "Let your skin dry before you get that suit back on. It's warm because it doesn't breathe well."

"Thank you." Hope turned so she faced the fire, holding out her hands to its warmth. The curved tops of her breasts were exposed. Most of her hair was still in one long braid that fell down her back, but tendrils had escaped around her face and down her nude shoulder blades, tickling the generous swell of her breasts.

Breath froze in Charlie's throat. His cock hadn't retreated much from its earlier arousal, and it jerked in his pants as desire cascaded through him. He wanted the woman crouched by the fire. Wanted her with a vengeance that defied both wisdom and reason. If Frank hadn't been there…

As if the other man were tuned in to Charlie's thoughts, Frank straightened and looked right at him. "I called Langley like you said. Was about to radio these coordinates, but I wanted your opinion. Do you think that flat spot across the creek is good enough for a landing zone?"

Charlie blanked his mind of Hope's hair and eyes and shoulders and breasts and the dark, secret mysteries between her legs. His lack of professionalism disgusted him. Men who were easily distracted in the field ended up dead. He'd seen it happen and prided himself on never being one of the rubes who let their dicks lead them around.

"Hang on," he told Frank. "Let me take a look. Even with the injections, my night vision isn't as good as yours."

Welcoming the chance to tear his gaze from Hope still holding her hands to the blaze, he clambered down the bank and picked his way across the partially frozen creek. With help from his penlight, he surveyed what turned out to be a marginal landing site.

"Frank. Get over here and help me move some of these rocks. Did you get an ETA for the bird?"

"Not yet." The other man joined him. "I wasn't going to radio back until we determined if a helicopter could land here. I thought it would be dicey, but doable."

"You thought right, but we can make it less dangerous if we clear the bigger rocks out of the way."

He bent to the task of chucking rocks off to the side. Gloves would've been nice, but the freaks had taken his backpack. As he thought about it, he'd been damned lucky they hadn't taken his clothes. It would've been smarter because he'd have had a much harder time escaping into New England's winter weather.

Yeah. Dumb shits even left me my boots.

"I'm sure I broke some kind of normal human rules here by helping myself to your thoughts," Frank's voice rumbled, "but it's a mistake to underestimate my erstwhile kin. We don't think the same way you do, but that doesn't make us any less deadly an enemy."

Charlie heaved a twenty-five pound rock aside and straightened. "You're right. Sorry. People with my background receive standardized training in war zone tactics. Part of that includes thinking ahead and doing everything you can to disable your opponent."

"They did," Frank said. "They put you in a shielded room where no one could find you and latched you to concrete blocks with wrist shackles. Had you been who they assumed, you'd still be there."

"I can help," Hope called as she joined them.

Charlie's heart did a funny little gallop in his chest, and he looked her way. She was zipped back into her flight suit, hood in place, and a bright smile on her face.

Part of him was disappointed she was covered, but what the hell had he expected? For her to wend her way across the river with her breasts hanging out? It wasn't much more than ten degrees. His fingers probably had frostbite from handling the ice-coated rocks.

"Excellent. Three are fifty percent better than two." Charlie kept his voice upbeat and hoped neither freak was in his mind. "I'll raise Langley and update them with these coordinates. Dawn's not far off, so we should be out of here soon."

"I'll believe it when it happens," Hope said.

"Even if a freak or two stayed," Frank cut in, "it won't be enough to sabotage an aircraft. Takes a whole lot of us to do that."

"How does that work, exactly?" Charlie asked. "Tell me once I'm off this call." Tapping his display, he radioed Langley.

He turned to Frank and Hope after he was done. "Great news. Chopper took off ninety minutes ago. It'll be here in about forty-five minutes. Now tell me more about the Vulcan mind meld."

"Excuse me?" Frank heaved a rock aside and straightened, facing Charlie.

"Sorry. Just a saying."

"It's from the old TV show, *Star Trek*," Hope cut in. "Spock was a Vulcan. They were kind of like us. Totally rational and able to blend mind power to make things happen."

"Found it." Frank nodded. "Part of accessing data in my brain is knowing how it's categorized. Not that we're anything like mythical aliens, but ten of us can bring down an aircraft. Fifteen makes it easier, and twenty would make it trivial. We focus our kinetics on the same wavelength and aim it at whatever we want to interrupt. All your modern aircraft run on computers, so we merely disrupt it by inserting competing commands."

"You instruct the computer to pilot the craft into the ground?" Charlie inhaled sharply. It was such a simple, yet elegant, sabotage, he admired the freaks for developing it.

"Precisely," Frank said. He made come along motions with both hands. "Well?"

"Well, what?" Charlie countered.

"What you should be asking is how to shield your aircraft from our interference."

The implication hit home and pinged a sour note. "If you knew how to do that and withheld information—" Charlie began.

"Stop right there," Frank said. "It's not wise to alienate someone offering assistance."

"Yeah," Hope chimed in. "This wasn't a big issue until yesterday's mission."

"Freaks took out my plane over the swamp," Charlie pointed out. "Milton's too."

"That's when I started thinking about how they might've done it," Frank noted. "It's not as if we've had much downtime between then and now. Look." He squared his shoulders and faced Charlie. "Either you trust us or you don't. Not much middle ground."

Kind of like with the lynxes. No middle ground with them, either.

"Touché." Charlie held out a hand. After a long moment, Frank grasped it. "Sorry, I was out of line."

"Wow! You apologized. Means there's hope for the truce between those of us who've defected and normal humans." Hope's green eyes glittered with a complex array of emotion. Optimism. Faith. Anticipation of a better future.

Charlie stared at her longer than he should have. If it were up to him, he'd make certain she was never disappointed again. Never mind, he understood how unrealistic that was.

"Let's finish these rocks." He bent and lifted another out of the landing area they were creating. Frank had been right to call him on his sudden attack of ambivalence. Hope, too. "While we're working, fill me in on how we can retrofit the planes so we're no longer vulnerable to attack."

"It won't be a hundred percent," Frank cautioned, "but if we add a device akin to the one that pumps out chaff, but make it specific to the computer…"

CHAPTER 6

*H*ope rolled over in bed and stretched her arms over her head. She loved her apartment on Langley's campus. Someone, Milton or Roy, had apologized for how small the women's quarters were, but it was the first time she'd had more than a narrow bunkbed for herself. At their compound, she'd shared a single room with eleven other women. To have any space at all that was hers and hers alone was unimaginable luxury, and her apartment included a living room, bedroom, kitchen, and bathroom. The first few weeks, she'd wandered from room to room lost in wonder that this sumptuous space was truly hers.

She burrowed deeper under the blankets that were another extravagance. At the compound, she'd slept beneath a single, thin coverlet with all her clothes on and still been cold. During particularly bad winters, the women had doubled up in their skimpy bunks for warmth.

Now that she was awake, her thoughts returned to that morning.

The helicopter had shown up within moments of them doing as much as they could to clear the field. She'd dozed most of the way back to Langley, and Charlie had given her and Frank the rest of the day off. He'd taken over as copilot on the jaunt back, so there hadn't been a chance for them to talk further.

She scrunched her eyes tight before opening them. Charlie had said they could continue their discussion, but she sensed his bone-deep ambivalence. He was attracted to her. She'd felt the sexual heat, first when he'd held her and then when he'd stared at her bare shoulders after Frank was done working on her cut places. Attraction was one thing, though. Wanting more than to drag her off to bed was something else altogether.

Maybe she could pump Charity for additional information from her foray into the CIA's personnel records. Why hadn't Charlie ever married again? Was there some deep, slimy secret he was afraid would surface?

Hope considered it. He wasn't gay, that was for damn sure. Or maybe he swung both ways. Sex at the compounds was forbidden, no matter who was involved, but she'd watched enough TV and spent enough time trolling the Internet to understand not everyone was wired exclusively male-female.

With her memory banks activated, she did a quick search. The majority of men who worked Black Ops weren't married. When she dug a little deeper, cops in general had higher divorce rates than the general population. Maybe the stress from their jobs—or the odd hours—were hard on marriages. Hope wished she knew more about normal humans. No amount of reading or TV watching could compensate for living in their midst, and she'd only been at Langley for a scant handful of months.

"Hey, hon, you awake?" Faith's query was soft, barely there so as not to disturb her.

"Yeah. Just getting up."

"If you toss on some clothes, we can catch last serving for supper in the cafeteria. I'm headed over there. Want me to stop by for you?"

"That'd be great. I'll hurry."

Hope tossed the blankets aside. It was dark outside her windows, which made sense. Eight p.m. was the latest they could show up for dinner. Snacks were available 24/7 because agents kept odd hours, but they weren't the same as sitting down to a hot meal.

The flight suit she'd worn for the better part of twenty-four hours lay crumpled on the floor. She could smell it from where she sat and crinkled her nose. It was warm and convenient since it was a one-piece zip up over long underwear, but she wasn't putting it back on until it could be laundered. She stood and trotted into the bathroom. A glance in the mirror revealed a face blotchy from sleep and hair spilling to her waist in a mass of tangles. She'd at least undone her braid before falling into bed.

The distant snick of a latch told her Faith had let herself in. The rooms were all outfitted with retinal scanners, but the women had reprogrammed them so they could get into each other's quarters. They'd meant to tell Milton or Roy or Charlie, but now that it was down to just her and Faith on the third floor in this particular women's apartment building, the topic didn't feel important enough to bother with.

"Hiya!" Faith joined her next to the sink and gave her a quick hug from the side. She was the same height as Hope and had the same long, black hair and green eyes. Shared genetic material went a long way toward making all the women look like sisters.

Hope bent and scooped lukewarm water from the taps, dipping her face into her cupped hands.

"Hiya, back." She grabbed a towel and blotted her streaming face.

"Rough time?" Faith looked her up and down. "Those are some hellacious wounds on your back. Looks like an animal mauled you. What the fuck happened?"

Hope rolled her eyes. "Those wounds are way better than right after it happened. Long story. If I tell you now, we'll miss dinner. Move over so I can grab some clothes."

"You can tell me over dinner. Charlie's been scarce all day. We've been practicing at the gun range and in the gym, but he hasn't surfaced since he showed up right after you all got back and told us to keep to the day's schedule."

Hope pulled a stretchy sweatshirt with a hood over her head. The CIA logo was emblazoned across its back. Next, she stepped into a pair of jeans and bent to stuff her feet into fur-lined winter boots.

"Your hair." Faith pointed. "You might want to run a brush through it."

Hope made a face. "Nah. It'll take too long." She scrunched handfuls together behind her head and secured the unruly mass with a rubber band. That done, she tugged her hoodie over everything. "There. No one will be able to see much." She grabbed a thick coat from a hook and put it on.

Faith held the door open for her. "I'm glad you're still here," she said and led the way down flights of stairs to ground level.

"I feel the same way about you," Hope replied. "I'm happy for Glory and Honor and Charity, but it's been kind of lonely since they moved in with their guys."

Cold air blasted through the door Faith had pushed open, and Hope strode outside to join her friend. "Brrr. Nippy tonight."

"Sure is. You know—" Faith lowered her voice conspiratorially "—Charity told us you were sweet on Charlie. You just got back from spending practically a whole day with him."

Hope ground to a halt. "So?" she demanded. Narrowing her eyes, she skewered her friend with a discerning glance. "Kind of puts a whole new spin on your dinner suggestion."

"I'm sure I have no idea what you mean. Come on." Faith tugged on her arm. "Too cold out here to not be moving."

"You and the other women want to know what happened. They all have men to go home to, so you drew the short straw. I bet you're supposed to report in before everyone hits the rack."

"We care about you," Faith protested. "It's not like we're a bunch of fuck ass gossips."

"Of course, we're a bunch of gossips," Hope retorted. Laughter bubbled from her. "We didn't have anything better to do in the compounds. Gossip was always a hot commodity." She removed a glove to place her palm on the reader plate next to the door in the cafeteria building. It swooshed open, and she and Faith walked through.

It always seemed odd to her that the scanner didn't slam the door shut on the next person, but maybe the CIA figured its agents were canny enough to not be hornswoggled into dragging an enemy into their midst. The cafeteria was housed in its own building. With enough seating to serve a hundred people, its interior was lined with many table and chair combos. The basic units seated four, but could be dragged together to accommodate much larger groups. Florescent lights cast a harsh, yellow glow over everything. The CIA dining room might be short on ambience, but the food was always plentiful and decently prepared.

"Hurry, you two," a man swathed in a white apron called. "I want to close the line and turn off the steam tables."

Hope rushed forward, grabbed a plate, and proceeded to pile it with everything in sight. Being bombarded with a bevy of food smells reminded her how hungry she was. Mercifully, Faith didn't mine for any more information until they were seated in a relatively quiet corner.

"What happened to your back?" Faith asked and began eating.

"The quick version is we went to ground in a mine. Freaks were tracking us and they dynamited the way we came in. I was hunting for an alternate way out—I'd found one too—but I disturbed a family of lynxes. I might've been able to placate them, but Frank and Charlie showed up—"

"I get it." Faith screwed her face into a frown. "Not exactly calming material. You're lucky you weren't cut up worse."

"Aw hell, I was mind-linked to both of them. Frank killed one, but I killed the one who landed on me, and I still feel like a murderess."

"It would've killed you," Faith protested.

"Yeah, but it had young."

"Ohhhh. What'll happen to them?"

Hope set her fork down. "Not sure. The men were convinced they were old enough to hunt on their own, so we left them there."

"Mmph." Faith cast an appraising glance her way. "Back to the men, those gashes looked pretty clean. Who did the honors?"

"What makes you think I didn't fix myself up?"

"We're wonder women, but even we can't see behind our backs. There wasn't so much as a speck of dirt left."

"You're impossible."

Faith winked broadly. "You didn't answer my question."

"What do you want to drink?" The cook who'd told them to hurry stopped by their table. His blond hair was cropped close to his head. Like most of the men in the CIA, he was tall and broad-shouldered with acres of muscles and a shrewd pair of eyes.

"Hot tea for me," Hope said. "I'd planned to get my own, but thanks."

"Same for me," Faith said. "No sugar for either of us."

"Yeah. I remember that part." The cook smiled at them. "I've had my eye on both of you for a while now. Either of you ladies doing anything later tonight?"

"Why?" Faith grinned back.

The cook shrugged, but didn't look the slightest bit embarrassed. "Well, couple of lookers like you. Thought you might be interested in maybe having drinks or something—back at my place."

"Both of us?" Hope's voice cracked.

Faith's grin faded. "Not a good idea."

"Why not?" He bent closer and lowered his voice. "We heard lots of stories about those compounds you used to live in. Thought maybe you might be lonely for the good, old days. There's plenty of me to go around." Sexual heat rolled off him in thick, nauseating waves.

Hope didn't need to glance down to know his white trousers were tented by an erection. Planting her palms flat on the table, she stood and stared at him. "Get lost, dude. We'll get our own tea."

"It's okay, honey. I like women who play hard to get. If you want me to slap you around a little, I like it rough too. We could have a blast—"

Hope didn't think. She drew back a fist and punched him hard. Blood spurted and he clapped a hand over his nose.

"Bitch!" He stalked off.

"Jesus, Hope. You broke his nose," Faith sputtered.

"Did not." She was breathing hard, and her appetite had vanished. She sank into her chair. "We probably should file a report before he beats us to it. He was gross, disgusting."

Faith trained troubled green eyes on her. "Do you suppose what he said is true? That they figure we had orgies at the compounds and we were just sitting ducks asking to get laid?"

"I have no idea." Hope shook her head. Weariness battered her in long, disquieting waves. "All I know is every single time I start to feel comfortable here in normal-human land, something like this happens and… Aw, shit!"

"What?" Faith swiveled her head around. "It's just Roy and Charlie."

Hope fisted a hand and pounded it on the table. "Yeah. Penis-boy probably reported us. Jesus, he was fast."

She got up again and loped to meet the men. "I can explain," she blurted. "At least I think I can."

Roy frowned. "Explain what? Charlie and I were picking up a late meal. Exactly what it looks like you and Faith are doing." When he looked at her, shockingly blue eyes crinkled at the corners. He had a square jaw, defined cheekbones, and a high forehead. Unkempt black hair fell to his collarbones. A couple inches taller than Charlie, Roy was built like a well-muscled athlete. Both men were dressed in dark pants and CIA sweatshirts with shoulder holsters and weapons casually tossed atop them.

"Yeah, it's exactly what we were doing." Faith joined them. "Until that dickwad of a cook propositioned both of us."

"What?" Charlie's face darkened into a thundercloud, and he drew his brows into a single, thick line. "What happened?"

"Basically, he said he'd heard the compounds were nothing but hot and cold running sex, and he wanted to resurrect the fond memories we must have—by inviting both of us to screw him," Faith gritted out. "Fucker."

"I hit him," Hope said. "Punched him, actually. Sorry. I didn't mean to, but he pissed me off."

The corners of Roy's mouth twitched, but he didn't laugh. "I'm on it. Go back to your food before it gets cold."

"Not very hungry," Hope muttered.

"Eat!" Charlie barked. "That's an order. Roy and I will join you once we're done with the cook." He bolted after Roy, catching up to him when he disappeared through the swinging door into the kitchen.

"Come on." Faith walked back to what was left of their cooling dinners. "Wonder what they'll do to him?"

"Doesn't matter." Hope fell into her chair, picked up a fork, and started eating again. Her stomach was tied in knots, but she forced food down anyway, chewing and swallowing mechanically.

Faith worked her way through a few mouthfuls before she said, "Of course it matters. The men stood up for us."

"Don't you get it?" Hope stabbed the air with her fork. "We're different. This will underscore that. Lots of the humans here hate us. At best, we're a curiosity. At worst, they'd just as soon we were still relegated to compounds where we can't hurt them. I probably did break that jerk's nose. I didn't mean to hit him that hard, but we're strong. It's how we're made."

Faith nodded. "Yeah. I see. Or I think I do. This won't buy us any love, huh?"

"No. It won't."

Roy and Charlie crossed the room toward them with laden plates of their own. The men took the other two places at their table, but Roy didn't sit. "I'm going back for drinks. What'll it be?"

Hope snorted. "At one point, I'd asked for tea, but beer or wine would go better."

"Wine," Faith said and turned to Charlie. "What happened?"

Charlie shrugged. "Not much. He said you attacked him. We pressed the matter, and he caved. Nothing you need to worry about." He dug into his meal, eating quickly and efficiently.

Hope borrowed a page from him and finished the food on her plate. After years of short rations at the compound, she didn't have it in herself to waste so much as a crust of bread.

She was beginning to wonder what had happened to Roy, when he strode purposefully toward them. The cook walked behind him, hanging back. His nose had stopped bleeding, but it had an uneven aspect across the bridge. Hope sprang to her feet, hands extended, kinetic power balanced between her extended fingers.

"No closer," she warned.

"Hope." Roy's voice was sharp. "He's come to apologize. Stand down. Sheathe your power."

The cook's eyes widened. "Shit! Guess I'm lucky you didn't kill me." His features creased in macabre fascination. "You don't need weapons. How did you do that? Your hands were glowing. They still are."

Roy shot a look his way. "Not why I dragged you out here, Clark."

"Yes, sir." Clark snapped off a salute. "Sorry, ladies. I wasn't respectful. I hope you can forgive me."

"Of course," Faith muttered.

Hope dropped her hands to her sides. She should murmur some disclaimer and back off. Instead, she stalked closer. "You try living in a society that's foreign to you, where all you want is to blend in, but everyone keeps reminding you that you're a freak."

"I said I was sorry. Jesus, you're gorgeous when you're steamed."

"Enough!" Roy's voice could've etched glass. "Back to your duties."

"All I did was state what's true." Clark started toward the kitchen. "Hell," he tossed over one shoulder. "You married one of them, so you must agree."

"One more word out of you, and I'll institute disciplinary action for insubordination," Roy growled. Clark must've taken him seriously because he vanished into the kitchen.

"Sit." Charlie patted the table.

Hope trudged back to her place. "I've gotten up and down so much, I feel like a goddamned puppet."

"Yeah. Sorry about that. Did you get enough rest after we got back? Need you at a hundred percent on the flight line at zero six hundred tomorrow."

"I'll be there." His words piqued her interest. "What's up?"

"We're having a quick briefing at twenty-one hundred in Milton's conference room. It wasn't accidental Roy and I found you here. We were just killing two birds with one stone since we needed dinner."

"Soul of productivity, huh?" Hope tried not to smile, but felt her mouth curve anyway.

"Always." Charlie grinned back, the corners of his hazel eyes crinkling with amusement. "On a different topic, I can't say much more about this, but we identified the problem that sabotaged our last mission, and—"

"Nope. Stop right there. Classified." Roy took his seat and ate just as efficiently as Charlie, whose plate was empty.

"I wasn't going to say much more," Charlie protested.

"It's okay. We've already forgotten. Back to the cook, Faith and I were going to file an incident report as soon as we were done eating," Hope said, still stiff and uncomfortable from her run-in with the man. For someone who wasn't supposed to indulge in feelings, she'd fallen prey to a whole host of them lately.

Roy set his fork down and drained half a can of beer. "I'm only going to say this once. Glory's heard it from me, so you need to as well. Assimilation takes time. A year from now, most—but not all— of the folk here will be used to you. They won't see you as a circus sideshow attraction or as something to be feared."

"Not going to happen overnight," Charlie concurred. Something crossed his face, but was gone before Hope could begin to interpret it. He glanced at a clock high on one wall. "We're due in ten for that briefing."

"So we are." Roy pushed away from the table and stood. "Come on, Charlie. See you gals over there."

"Right behind you." Charlie loped after Roy's departing form.

Hope got to her feet too, waiting for Faith. "You've been quiet."

"Not much to say. Mostly I was paying attention to how Charlie looked at you."

Hope hustled toward a different exit than the one the men had taken. The absolute last thing she wanted was to dissect her confusing welter of emotions where Charlie was concerned. They'd fallen back into the comfortable place they'd carved out earlier while bantering around the table. She'd been afraid he'd be disgusted or disappointed by her run-in with the cook, but it seemed to amuse him more than anything else.

Faith joined her. "Aren't you going to ask me what I saw?"

"I have a feeling you're going to tell me anyway." Hope turned to her friend as they broke into a trot to cover the mile between them and the building that housed Milton's office and conference rooms.

"He likes you. I sensed him wishing there were more between you and—"

"Stop right there." Hope clamped her jaws together. "You mined data from his thoughts."

Exactly like I did earlier. Just because we can doesn't make it right.

"So, sue me. He didn't know. He was so focused on you, he wasn't paying one whit of attention to me."

Data bits slammed into a whole like puzzle pieces clicking into place, and she understood the flash of uneasiness she'd picked up from Charlie after Roy's impromptu speech. Or she thought she did.

"Charlie's one of the ones who doesn't totally trust us," she said dully.

"You're wrong. I did not pick that up from his thoughts," Faith insisted. "That thing he alluded to when Roy cut him off?"

"Yeah?"

"That's what they were dancing around with all that assimilation talk. I bet they found one of their own who sabotaged your last mission. It's what Charlie meant when he said they'd fixed the problem and Roy shut him up."

"Do you really think so?"

Faith nodded. "I do indeed. Plus it fits with what I skimmed from his mind."

Hope hesitated, but it was better to keep talking. Faith was her friend. She wouldn't betray confidences. "Charlie wants me. I turn him on. I want him that way too, but it's better if we don't go down that street."

"Why?" Faith asked. "Glory and Honor and Charity are happy."

"Charity hooked up with a Nameless One," Hope pointed out.

"Erg. That's worse in so many ways. Remember how much agony she went through before she gave in and accepted that Tony was the only one for her?"

Hope did remember, and it hadn't been pretty. "I still think Charlie doesn't trust us. Not entirely. He wants to, but there's some innate reticence. Plus, how come he never remarried?"

"Why don't you ask him? Whatever it is, I'm certain it has nothing to do with us."

Hope almost choked. "Way too personal. I'd never ask him something like that."

"I could sort through his mind, kind of like I did tonight. Or I could hack into the CIA personnel database same as Charity did and report back."

Hope wrapped an arm around Faith. They were almost at the building, which meant they'd have to stop talking. "Promise me. Do nothing."

"Okay, but why? You said you needed information. If it's the only thing standing between you and true love…"

"I love you, hon. Many reasons for you not to do either of those things. First off, we work for the CIA. It means we follow their rules. Next, I'm ambivalent about how I feel about Charlie too. He's not the only one who's conflicted. It's not as if you could come up with some prime piece of info that would change my mind."

She stopped in front of a side door, waiting before she activated the retinal scanner that would disengage the locking mechanism. "I appreciate your concern, but this thing between Charlie and me will either develop on its own—or not. It's not something you can hurry along with kinetics."

Faith hugged her and tilted her head to activate the scanner. "I was only trying to help. Actually, I don't want to be the only one left in our apartment building."

"You won't be. Come on. I'm curious what the men have hatched up for our next move."

"Me too, but I'm not very happy we weren't included in that discussion. You were asleep, but they could've dragged the rest of us out of practice."

Hope didn't reply right away. She took the stairs three at a time. Like most of the Langley buildings, this one had elevators, but she didn't care for them. When she got to the corridor that led to the conference room, she turned to Faith. "They may not have included us at the front end, but that conversation was likely between Milton, Roy, and Charlie. They do ask for input at these briefings."

"You're right." Faith smiled warmly. "Sorry to be bitchy. This is way better than the compounds. The Nameless Ones treated us like yesterday's trash."

The idea of a Nameless One asking their opinions about anything struck Hope as funny in a black humor kind of way, and she started to laugh.

"What's so funny?" Charity called from inside the meeting room.

"Nothing. Good to see you." Hope made her way to where the women sat on their usual side of the room. "How's Tony?"

"You can ask me," Tony's voice boomed from back by the coffee pot. "I'm right here."

"So, how are you?" Hope flashed a grin his way.

"Better than good. Coffee?"

"Thanks, but I'm good for now."

Milton Reins, head of the CIA's covert operations units, strode to the front of the room. He was dressed in dark trousers, a rumpled white shirt, and a dark tie that he'd dragged open. Salt and pepper hair fell to his shoulders, and he scanned the room with shrewd, dark eyes that missed very little. "Seats, everyone. Now. We got another shot at that Cortexiphan, and we're going to move on it. Not because we can't synthesize our own, but because I'll be goddamned if I'll leave it for the freaks to make themselves stronger."

CHAPTER 7

Charlie listened with half an ear as Milton outlined their strategy for tomorrow. Earlier, they'd triangulated the spot Charlie was held prisoner, which corroborated that the second compound near Bangor was still alive and kicking.

Two fighter jets would drop C4 canisters before dawn to obliterate the compound and as many freaks as they could. Once they were done, helicopters would deliver two squads on the ground where they could mop up, secure the Cortexiphan, and fly back to Langley.

For once, Frank waited until Milton was done before he raised a hand.

"Yeah?" Milton eyed him.

"Couple of problems, but before that, did you figure out how freaks found out about our last mission and nailed two of our choppers?"

"Sure did. It's been handled."

Frank eyed Milton speculatively. "Are you going to say more about that?"

"If I was, I'd still be talking. What are those problems you alluded to?"

"Alrighty, then. First one is we have no idea where they've stored the drug. It might not be located at the compound. Next one is we're not offering amnesty opportunities before we bomb the fuck out of that compound."

Glory turned his way. "We kind of did," she said. "Milton and Roy put those flyers together weeks ago, and they got a lot of airtime. It's how you and Tony found out about it."

"You're assuming everyone in the compounds got a look at the amnesty offer," Tony spoke up. "Only reason Frank and I saw it was because we had an autonomous lab where no one bothered us, and no one censored our feed. They couldn't because we needed full data access for our genetic work."

"This is essentially the same operation we pulled off in the swamp," Milton argued. "We offered amnesty afterward—got a few takers as I recall. I'm more concerned about the Cortexiphan. Why do you believe they'll conceal it?" Breath hissed from between his teeth. "We can't offer amnesty before we move in. If we did, they'd relocate the drug for certain."

Charlie pushed to his feet and sent a pointed glance Frank's way. "What was that deal about V4 proving unstable and them needing you to fix it?"

"You mean the conversation we had with the freaks when they were outside the lead mine?"

"Yes."

"Tony and I appreciate how unstable V4 is," Frank began. "We understood that before we left. Apparently the others are coming to the same conclusion."

"Yeah," Tony spoke over him. "It's why I made the decision to not use Cortexiphan—or any other drug—to keep working on our genome. V3 is good enough. We can live with it. We know its strengths and its weaknesses, and we can fix it when it goes south."

"Your point?" Milton pressed, sounding exasperated. "It's late."

"Cortexiphan is hard to synthesize," Frank said. "Not for us in our current situation, but it wasn't easy to get hold of the requisite components in the compounds. We had to steal them, usually from closely guarded chemical supply companies."

"That drug is currently the primary element in our arsenal to deal with any and all types of malfunctions," Tony added. "Because of that, we viewed it as a lifeline and parceled it out sparingly. You can bet if the freaks in that compound feel the least bit threatened, the first thing they're going to sequester is the Cortexiphan. It's right up there with programming the mainframe running the show to implode if they're attacked."

Milton clicked a few buttons, and the wall display behind him lit with a schematic. "Charlie, is this how the compound was laid out?"

"Near as I could tell," Charlie replied.

"They're all the same," Tony said. "Except for the one in the swamp, and it was different for a whole lot of reasons. It was designed as a headquarters. Only men lived there, and the computers were all above ground because seepage made subterranean rooms impossible to construct and maintain."

"Does anyone have any better ideas for how to structure tomorrow?" Milton's steely, dark eyes moved around the room.

The pilot and copilot for each fighter jet lounged near the back of the room. They had the easy job, and hopefully they'd remain airborne. Frank's explanation of how to shield the onboard computers from sabotage had been simple enough to implement—even with short notice.

Milton finished his visual transit of the room. "Hearing none, we're going with the plan I laid out. Quarters, men. Flight line at zero six hundred for ground teams, zero four thirty for the jets."

"Got it, sir." The fighter jet crews murmured in a chorus. The four men rose as a unit and loped from the room.

"What are the rest of you waiting for?" Milton furled his brows. "We'll sort out who goes in which chopper on the flight line. Be sure to stop by the armory. Full field regalia. Extra clips."

Charlie held back while everyone filed out.

Milton turned to him. "What is it?"

"Got a few moments, sir?"

Milton grunted and strode to the door, kicking it shut. He turned to face Charlie. "Spit it out, McClaren. Did something happen on that mission you neglected to tell me about?"

Charlie's face heated and he raked his hands through his unkempt hair. "I'm sorry about this, sir—"

"For Christ fucking sake, just tell me. Save the apologies for later. What's eating you enough to lose sleep over it?"

Charlie inhaled unevenly but forced himself to stand razor straight. "It's Hope, sir."

"What about Hope? Do you have reason to believe she's a spy? Was she the conduit between our man, who's in lockdown and facing a court-martial, and the freak compound?"

Charlie fell back a pace. Out of all Milton's possible reactions, he hadn't anticipated this one. "No, sir. Not at all, sir. I— That is, well, I seem to be more interested in her than I should be. I know we just restructured our teams because of Roy and Glory, but maybe it's better if Hope doesn't report to me."

Milton narrowed his eyes and drew his silver brows into a line that cut low across his forehead. "How far has this gone, McClaren?"

"Nowhere, sir. So far, it's only in my head. Maybe hers. I have no idea how she feels, but after the lynx landed on her, I was inappropriate. I held her when there was no reason."

Milton chuckled. "I assume she didn't haul off and slap you or wriggle to get out of your arms. She sure as hell didn't break your nose, and we've established she's capable of that."

"No, but she was in shock."

A long, rippling sigh rustled from Milton's throat. "These women do not go into shock, McClaren. If she didn't like it right where she was, she'd have made it abundantly clear."

Emotion flooded Charlie, bombarding him with possibilities. "Do you really think she might care about me?"

"I'm damn near certain of it, son. Circling back to your

personnel-juggling request, it's a bit late in the game for tomorrow, but I can make certain she's part of Kincaid's squadron. We'll save a more permanent solution for later."

Reality caught up with Charlie, and his elation receded. "Might be premature, sir. I really have no idea if she—"

"Do I look like Dear Abby? Get moving. Unless there's some other prime tidbit you need to drop in my lap before we deploy tomorrow."

"No, sir. No other tidbits, prime or otherwise." Charlie turned and bolted from the room. Happiness spilled through him. If Milton were convinced Hope liked him, maybe she really did. He let himself out one of the building's many side doors into a cold, foggy night. Frost coated everything in sight, making the ground slick in places, but he broke into a run anyway.

His cock had been doing nothing but giving him grief since he'd held Hope in his arms. Jacking off had done less than nothing to mute his desire for her, and despite his quick pace, his dick swelled again, pressing against the front of his trousers.

He spared a thought for the cook who'd had the temerity to proposition Hope and wanted to finish pounding his face to dog meat. Hope might have broken his nose, but Charlie could black both eyes, break his cheekbones…

And get myself court-martialed for attacking a fellow employee.

He skidded to a halt in front of a building and realized with a start that it wasn't his quarters, but Hope's apartment complex. His cock throbbed with anticipation. His brain was mush with wanting to crush her against him, bury his hands in her long, dark hair, and taste her firm lips. A vision of her bare shoulders and the upper curves of her breasts blasted into his mind.

His cock jerked in his pants. Charlie's breath steamed white in the frosty air. If he did knock on her door, no way he could show up in his current state with the front of his pants sticking out. He slithered away from the building and its phalanx of brilliant outdoor lighting—never mind its cameras—and lost himself in the shadows of a grove of deciduous trees.

Grappling with his zipper, he worked his cock free. It quivered in his palm, hot, hard, and ready. Charlie stopped thinking. He closed a hand around himself and stroked quick and hard. He knew what he needed, what he had to have. A naked Hope burst into his mind in all the glory he imagined. High breasts, puckered nipples, slick heat between her thighs. He imagined he was pushing into her, feeling the scorching center of her body tighten around him.

He stroked himself harder, faster. She wanted him too, told him how she longed for his touch, needed him to take her. Semen jetted from him, and he kept coming for long, tantalizing moments. He'd come so fast, it was unsettling. Surely, he'd be able to modulate his body's reactions better with an actual partner. It had been long enough, though, he wasn't certain. He was still idly stroking himself, and he forced himself to quit. He'd done this for a reason: so he could show up at Hope's door. He'd never meant to stand outside like some pervert diddling himself. His erection had deflated, but not by much. He managed to stuff himself back into his pants, still sucking air.

A quick jog around that quadrant of Langley got his breathing back to normal. He had a fighting chance of being rational when he knocked on Hope's door.

What if she was asleep?

He frowned. Maybe this wasn't such a good idea. They had a big day tomorrow, and everyone needed rest.

I'm a fucking coward. First I can't talk with her because I'm too aroused. Now I'm worried about sleep. Shit! She slept most of the day.

Before he could argue himself out of it, Charlie tilted his chin so the building's scanner would admit him. He nodded at the night sentry pacing back and forth in the lobby and ducked into the stairwell. The women lived on the third floor. As he climbed the stairs, he shuffled through what he would say.

What possible excuse could he have for knocking on her door at ten at night?

He shook his head. No excuses. He'd tell her the truth and see where it went. This wasn't the time or place for games. He liked her. If she returned his feelings, maybe they could get to know each other better.

Damn. That sounded stilted and hokey as hell. This wasn't boy meets girl circa the year two thousand. They were embroiled in a war zone. Surely the gradual, get-to-know-you games weren't relevant anymore. Particularly since normal humans and freaks had played on opposite teams for the last seven years.

He'd been standing in front of her door for several minutes, trying out and discarding greetings. Thank God the hallway was empty. It would be, though, since Faith and Hope were the only residents on this floor. He raised his hand to knock, and then let it fall to his side.

Charlie felt disgusted with himself. If he couldn't gin up enough balls to declare his presence, he should leave.

The door whooshed open, shocking him. Hope stood swathed in a pale blue robe. Loose dark hair flowed down her shoulders to waist level. She leveled her gaze at him. "You've been standing out here for ten minutes. What do you want?"

He started to blunder through asking how she'd known, but was smart enough to keep his mouth shut. She'd no doubt felt his energy pulsing on the far side of her door.

She crossed her arms under her breasts, enhancing their outline through the thin, silky fabric of her robe. "What do you want?" she asked again.

"May I come in?"

Hope shrugged and stepped aside. "Sure. It's a mess."

"I'm not the greatest housekeeper myself."

Charlie walked past her and around a couple piles of discarded gear. The apartment smelled like her, honeysuckle and orange, with undernotes of cinnamon. It was all he could do not to inhale noisily. He turned to face her. "I'm sorry for disturbing you."

She waved him to silence. "I work for you. That means you don't have to apologize. Was there some change in tomorrow's plans?"

"No. No change, and this isn't exactly about work."

A wary look crossed her face, not unlike expressions he'd seen on caged animals. "Is it about what I did to the cook?" She looked away. "I know my temper can run hot. I'll do a better job controlling it. Promise. Maybe there's some kind of healing I could do with my kinetics to repair his nose faster."

"Hope. It's not about him. It's about me." Charlie ground his teeth together. "Look, I'm not very good at stuff like this. I—I'm attracted to you. I've tried to fight it, but it's been going on for a while now. When I held you earlier, it was really presumptuous of me. I'm sorry if I crossed a boundary. Didn't mean to, but you're so beautiful, I couldn't help myself."

He'd been watching her closely, ready to stammer excuses and bolt out the door the moment she looked disgusted or bored or like she pitied him. None of that happened. Her eyes kindled with something he didn't exactly have a name for, but they burned like green flames, warm and welcoming.

The corners of her mouth twitched with amusement. "You saw what happened to a guy who crossed one of my boundaries. Last time I checked, your nose is intact. So's the rest of you."

Charlie felt like jumping up and down and whooping like a fool, but it paid to double-check these things. "What are you saying, Hope?"

She held out her arms, and the silky fabric of her robe stretched tighter across her breasts.

Charlie didn't wait for her to spell it out. He dove into her embrace and wrapped his arms around her, holding her close. Too late, he remembered his layers of winter clothing, but none of that mattered. The only thing that did was the magic of the woman looking at him out of her clear, green eyes.

"I've never kissed a man before. You'll have to teach me."

He brushed his thumb over her lips. "I'd be delighted. And I'm more than thrilled to be the first man to kiss you."

"Well, it's a good thing one of us knows something, although Charity and Tony managed okay."

"I'm not surprised. It's kind of like breathing." Charlie kissed her once softly, experimentally, letting his lips rest atop hers. He teased her lips with his alternating little biting kisses with small licking kisses, careful to let her set the pace.

She kissed him back, moving her hands until they splayed across his shoulders. The swell of her breasts pressed against his chest, and he felt her nipples harden into tight balls even through his heavy jacket. Urgency raced through him. In the years since his marriage imploded, he'd taken care of his sexual desires with women who demanded nothing. Sometimes he paid them; sometimes not, but sex had turned into a simple act. No emotion. Just pure, physical release. He wanted more with Hope. Much more, which meant taking things slow.

She pressed the length of her body against him and broke their kiss. A lazy smile lightened her features, turning her into something so beautiful, breath clotted in his throat.

"You feel good," she murmured, her voice a low, throaty purr. "If that's what kissing is all about, I want more of it."

"That makes two of us." He cradled her tenderly, careful to avoid the places high on her shoulders where the cat had nailed her. "How are your wounds?"

"Healing. We heal fast. Probably because we can direct our native kinetic energy where we need it most."

Charlie trailed his fingertips down one side of her face and looped hair behind her ear. "You're lovely. I could look at you forever."

"You're not bad, yourself. When you forget about being a big, tough warrior and let yourself smile."

"I'll keep it in mind."

Because he couldn't resist, he angled his head and kissed her again. This time, he teased her lips with his tongue, pressing until she opened her mouth to him. He slid his tongue inside, delighted when she sucked on it. Plus it made him hotter than hell.

She ground her hips against his lower body and had to feel the bulge of his erection. Charlie congratulated himself for having had the presence of mind to take the edge off his lust with his hand before showing up here. If he hadn't done that, holding himself back from carting Hope to her bedroom would have been damn near impossible.

It was hard enough, as it was.

She moaned low in the back of her throat, still kissing him as if the world would stop spinning on its axis if they let go of one another.

He threaded his hands beneath her hair and held her head steady while he plumbed her mouth with deep, hungry kisses. The distant vibration of his wrist computer nagged.

Aw shit. Not now.

He was a soldier first, though, and had been for enough years he couldn't ignore the summons. He pulled away from her, mumbled, "Sorry," and brought the device to eye level.

"You all right, sir?" flashed across his screen.

He typed back, "Yes, home soon."

"What was that about?" Hope asked.

Charlie still held her in the circle of his arms. "You know how you have a night sentry downstairs?" At her nod, he continued. "All the buildings have them. That was mine. Part of his job is making sure everyone is accounted for. I didn't file a report on my whereabouts after the briefing, and it's been over for a while."

Hope cocked her head to one side. "Maybe where we stopped is good for now?"

"It is." He cupped the side of her face in one hand. "If we get back early enough tomorrow, we could have dinner together."

"I'd like that." She closed her teeth over her lower lip. "What about all that line of command shit? Glory couldn't work for Roy. If we're going to, um, date, how will that work?"

Charlie ducked away from her direct gaze and settled for looking askance at her. "I might have already covered that with Milton. After tonight's briefing."

"Might have?" She smothered something that sounded like a giggle.

He shrugged and borrowed a page from her book. "I'll never tell. I wasn't sure then if you were interested in me, so I told Uncle Miltie it might be premature, but—"

She placed the flat of her hand over his mouth. "I love it that you cared enough to bring it up. Means you're serious about me, and I'm not something you want to hide." Hope took a breath before continuing. "It also means you're not ashamed of wanting to be with me. That means a whole lot. I knew you wanted to have sex with me, but I didn't think there was any more to it than that."

He met her gaze. "There's way more than just sex here, Hope. I haven't let a woman into my life since my divorce fifteen years ago, but I want you. I've thought about you pretty much nonstop since I first laid eyes on you, but we can have that conversation tomorrow after we get back. For now, get good rest. The days when we slaughter your people can't be easy for you."

"I feel bad for the women," she admitted. "In terms of the Nameless Ones, meh. They're getting about what they deserve. You'd never know it from Frank and Tony and the other guys who've defected, but most of them were assholes. They loved lording it over us." She looked away. "I don't want to talk about them. You're going to have to let go of me before you can leave."

"My practical darling." He brushed his lips over hers one last time before disentangling himself.

"Maybe over dinner you can tell me more about yourself." Her eyes gleamed with genuine interest that warmed him from his head to his toes.

"If it'll save you hacking into our database, I'd be glad to."

"See what comes of telling you my secrets? You toss them in my face. Good night, Charlie. I'm glad you came by."

"Night, Hope. Me too. It wasn't easy."

"Big, tough warrior like you?"

Charlie snorted. "Yeah, warriors don't have to deal with slippery concepts like how to tell a woman she's gorgeous or that we think about her all the time. Much easier to chuck a grenade into a building and be done with it."

"Maybe so. Well, you can get the grenade chucking out of your system tomorrow."

"And clear the decks for us." He headed for the door before he lost the willpower to leave.

She followed him and opened it. "I like the sound of that. I'll hold you to clearing those decks."

Charlie walked out the door and down the hall, so high on what had just happened, he couldn't quite believe it. Hope did care about him. Now if they could just get through tomorrow…

He stopped outside her building thinking about tomorrow's mission. What they did was extremely dangerous. He loved the adrenaline high. It was what had driven him first into the Seals and then into the CIA. Problem was everyone else was cut from the same cloth. The women weren't known to go to the mat to protect themselves. None of the freaks did. It was why they were perfectly cast as CIA agents.

He'd just opened his heart for the first time in a long time, though, and it shaded how he viewed the world.

"Nothing will happen to her," he growled. "Not a damn thing. I'll see to it."

How the hell will I finesse that if she's in Roy's squadron?

Protectiveness raced through him. He wanted Hope next to him where he could keep an eye on her, but his military training screamed it was the wrong move. If he focused the lion's share of his attention on the woman he'd just left, it wouldn't be fair to the rest of his team.

Or to the other squadron they were working alongside.

I'll figure it out. Roy and Milton did, which means I'll come up with a compromise.

Somehow.

With a last glance upward at the window he knew was hers, he blew her a kiss. She'd never know, but he did.

CHAPTER 8

Hope made her way to the flight line half an hour early. Sleep had been elusive, mostly because she'd replayed every word, every kiss, every touch from Charlie's visit, savoring the moments as she relived them. Part of her was sorry she hadn't dragged him into her bedroom, but maybe normal human women weren't that forward. She wanted him to respect her, not see her as a sex-starved slut.

She smothered an amused snort. Of course she was sex-starved, and if wanting to rip the clothing off his body so she could see what a man looked like up close and personal was slutty behavior, then she was one of them too.

It was cold in the predawn gloom, and the damp sank into her bones with every breath. While not entirely healed, her shoulders didn't ache like they'd done at this time yesterday. She took a quick inventory. She had her AK-47, a nine-millimeter sidearm, and enough ammunition to sink a boat. She'd also tucked several grenades into her rucksack. The man in the armory had been delighted to have something to do. She hadn't had any competition at five a.m.

A quick check of her internal clock told her it was quarter to six, and everyone else should come filing in soon. Their two CH-47F Chinooks had just fired up their rotors, and they spun lazily.

Faith hustled into the huge hangar. "There you are! I looked for you, but you'd already left."

Hope turned toward her friend. "Sorry. I would've rousted you, but I was up really early, and I didn't want to bother you."

"Hey, gals!" Glory loped over to them, her breath making clouds in the cold air.

"Hey, yourself," Hope countered. "Ready to do this?"

"You betcha!" Glory grinned. "One of these days, the freaks will see reason, and we can put this war behind us."

"Wouldn't that be nice?" Faith sounded wistful.

"Wouldn't what be nice?" Honor joined them with Charity right behind her.

"A world where everyone liked each other." Glory beamed at the other four women. "It would mean Roy and I would never have to get out of bed."

"Ha! Yeah and I want a unicorn for my birthday, but staying in bed with Tony would have its plusses." Charity laughed, but it held grim undernotes.

"We don't exactly have birthdays," Hope reminded her, sidestepping the blatant allusion to sex.

"Oh yeah, huh." Charity's usual sarcasm was back in spades. "On a more practical note, do you suppose we'll get to the women in this compound before the Nameless Ones massacre them?"

"I sure hope so," Hope said. "I remember that one mission where the bodies were still warm. Made me sad the Nameless Ones hated us that profoundly. There was no reason to kill those women—other than to keep them away from safe haven with us."

"Emotion is not where we live," Honor reminded her. "Don't get sad, get even."

Hope snapped off a salute. "Yes, ma'am."

"That's captain, ma'am, to you," Honor retorted. "Or colonel or general. Take your pick."

"If you're gonna dream, dream big," Glory broke in.

"Eyes this way," Milton boomed.

Hope spun so she faced the front of the hangar. She hadn't expected Milton. He hadn't gone on a mission since his near brush with death, but judging from his flight suit, he was coming on this one. In addition to the five genetically altered women, fifteen men fanned around where Milton stood.

"Excellent." Milton nodded sharply. "Ten minutes to departure. The jets are about an hour from their targets. By the time we arrive an hour after that, the fires should've died down enough for us to locate spots to land. We'll pack ten in a bird. Roy and Charlie will pilot the first craft. David and I will take the other one. Your team leaders today are Roy and myself. Honor and Charity will be in Roy's chopper and on his team. Glory, Hope, and Faith will be with me. Men, split up so half go in each chopper."

"Means we get to choose, right?" Frank angled a brow.

Milton narrowed his eyes. "Glad you asked. Tony will go with me. You'll join Roy. Everyone else can sort out which team they want to be part of. Questions?"

Milton allowed a scant five seconds. When no one spoke up, he said, "Go. Let's get this mission buttoned up. Each bird is carrying specialized equipment to locate the drug. Assuming we get lucky, and it hasn't left in a car or plane for points unknown."

"Two hours flight time?" one of the men asked.

"Roughly. Depends on winds aloft," Roy answered.

Hope thought about the big choppers. They'd need to refuel before returning. She searched her database brain, but didn't locate any military bases that were still open in the area. Guess that meant they'd end up at Bangor International Airport, which wasn't the end of the world.

She was thinking about refueling as a diversionary tactic, as if future projecting would protect her from the next few hours. Stumbling over another bunch of women who'd been murdered wasn't high on her list. It made it hard to be civil to Frank, Tony, and the other Nameless Ones who'd defected. Not that they'd been directly responsible for the women's plight in the compounds, but nor had they stood up to the status quo, demanding it be changed.

As if thinking about him had drawn him, Tony poked her in the back, but well below her injuries. "Get moving, Hope." His voice was gruff.

She didn't bother answering, just loped onto the tarmac and headed for the chopper that would carry them north to their next confrontation. Tony was right behind her, but something about his energy felt off to her.

"You okay?" She glanced over one shoulder.

"Fine. I really look forward to killing my erstwhile kin." He pushed around her and bounded up the steps, cutting off the possibility of further conversation.

Hope made her way into the utilitarian interior of the bird and strapped herself into a hard seat bolted to one wall. These choppers had been built to move far bigger payloads than a dozen people, and the bird's cavernous interior rose around her. Glory took the seat next to her, and Faith dropped into one on her other side. Hope settled her headset into place, and so did the other women.

Hope debated whether to have a heart-to-heart with Glory. The flight would last two hours, and they'd never have a better chance to talk. When they were at the base, Glory spent virtually all her off time with Roy, which made sense. This way, Hope could share her concerns—and her dreams—without feeling guilty about dragging the other woman away from the man she adored.

Faith would have to be part of the conversation, particularly if it took place using telepathy. Not that Hope couldn't shield telepathic communication, but Faith would know they were talking—even if she couldn't make out the words—and she'd feel left out.

The cabin vibrated as the rotors spun faster, heading for a speed that would lift them into the air. More to entertain herself than anything else, Hope tapped into the craft's computer, or tried to. Bursts of electrical interference stymied her, and she grinned.

"What's so funny?" Faith asked.

"Tried to eavesdrop on the computer, but that new chaff project kept me out."

"Good thing," Glory jumped into their conversation. "If you can't penetrate it, maybe the rest of us can't, either. Means our odds of remaining airborne just jumped into the ninetieth percentile."

Hope did a quick calculation of her own. Lots of things could interrupt their helicopter's forward trajectory. Wind shear. Birds. Electrical lines. Other aircraft. Mechanical failure. None of them were likely, but in aggregate, they meant no flight had an absolute guarantee of not running up against an unexpected event.

She waited until they were at cruise altitude and reached for the women on either side. Glory quirked a brow, but took her hand. Faith smirked. "I figured something was afoot when I couldn't find you this morning."

"Ssht." Hope switched to telepathy. It worked better and burned through far less kinetics when they were touching. It was why she'd reached for her sisters.

"Well?" Faith was almost bouncing up and down in her seat.

"At least try to look normal," Hope cautioned. *"Last thing we want is for the Nameless Ones to believe we're worth listening in on."*

"Got it." Faith settled against the hard back of her seat and crossed her legs.

"How did you figure out Roy was the one for you?" Hope asked Glory.

The other woman scrunched her forehead as she concentrated. *"It wasn't so much a single moment as a whole bunch of them that piled on top of one another until I couldn't ignore how much I liked him. I fought it for a long time. It was hard to trust he didn't have ulterior motives—kind of like the Nameless Ones—and if I dropped my guard, something terrible would happen."*

"But when did you know for sure?" Hope persisted.

"Not until after we got back to Langley." Glory rolled her eyes. *"Geez. He pretty much ignored me for a week. I was certain I'd imagined*

that he even liked me, but he was dealing with his own problems. One was having me in a direct line of command under him. Worse than that, though, his wife was executed in some kind of commando warfare. She wasn't an agent, but organized crime kidnapped her. He wasn't at all certain he wanted another woman he might lose to violence."

"You found a way around that, though. Right?" Faith jumped into the conversation. *"You must have."*

"Of course we did. Things got really good after I almost died in that cave-in, and he took me to this little hideaway in the San Juans once I was well enough to travel."

Faith poked Hope in the side. *"This must be about Charlie. Did he spend the night with you? Did you have sex? Did—?"*

"Stop it!" Hope poked her back. *"Yes he came to my room. No we did not have sex. We kissed and talked. It felt like...a beginning."*

"Awwww." Faith's green eyes shone with caring. *"I'm happy for you —even if it means there'll just be me left on our floor."*

"You're getting way ahead of the curve, sister." Hope tried to sound stern, but it didn't work very well.

"What exactly did he say?" Glory asked. *"Did the two of you plan to get together after the briefing?"*

"No. I was surprised when he showed up. Hell, he stood outside my door so long, I finally opened it."

"Didn't he knock?" Faith asked.

Hope shook her head. *"Nope. Just stood there, but I felt his energy pulsing, and I had no idea what he wanted, so I opened the door to ask."*

"Ever practical, that would be us." Glory laughed. At a sharp look from Tony, she rolled her eyes. "Fine," she directed words his way. "No more fun."

"It wasn't funny, not really," Hope went on. *"The longer Charlie stood there, the more nervous I grew. Faith knows this, but you might not. Earlier last night, I punched out one of the cooks who propositioned us. Broke his nose. I was afraid Charlie was standing outside my door trying to find a way to tell me I was done with the CIA, and that I'd have to leave."*

"What happened after you opened the door?" Faith asked.

"He looked really uncomfortable. It didn't make me feel any better. And then he asked if he could come inside."

"And?" Glory prodded. *"Don't make us dig this out of you. You're the one who asked for this conversation."*

Hope tried to conceal the smile that wanted out and ended up with what probably looked like a grimace. *"Charlie's a lot like us. Simple and direct. He just out and told me he liked me, and he hoped I felt the same."*

Two identical sets of green eyes stared at her; Hope stared back. *"That's about all, really. We kissed, and then he left."*

"Kissed? Why stop there?" Faith's mind voice was almost a squeal. She leaned closer and ran up against the confines of her seat harness.

Hope shrugged, suddenly uncomfortable. *"Not sure."* She turned to Glory. *"Does it not bode well that we weren't so hungry for each other, we couldn't hold back?"*

Glory squeezed her hand. *"Not at all, sweetie. The first time Roy kissed me, it was only one kiss. It scared the holy hell out of both of us. He went back to his room, and I bundled up and went outside into a storm. I was trying to keep him safe, and I sensed Nameless Ones closing on me."*

Relief streamed through Hope. "Thanks." She switched to regular speech.

"I'm guessing this means the private part of the discussion is done," Glory withdrew her hand after a final pat.

"But I want more details," Faith urged. "Juicy details for those of us who haven't been so lucky."

"Later." Hope grinned. "Once I have something more salacious to share."

"Salacious, eh?" One of the freaks she didn't know waggled his dark eyebrows. "Always told the guys that moratorium on sex was stupid."

"Not your conversation." Glory sent a pointed look his way.

"It's everyone's so long as we can hear," he countered. "Use shielded telepathy if you want to keep us out."

"We did," Faith shot back. "And it was dirty as hell. Put that in your pipe and smoke it."

The man rolled his amber eyes. "Cliché." He turned to Tony. "You've gotten laid, tell us about it."

"Stuff it, dude," Tony retorted. "If you want to talk about something, let's plan out what we'll do once we've got boots on the ground."

"No kidding about boots on the ground." Hope turned to Glory. "I was thinking earlier about the chance you took rescuing us that night in our compound. If I never thanked you, I'm thanking you now. I still feel rotten about the seven of us who ignored your warning—and your offer of freedom."

"Aw, hon." The corners of Glory's eyes pinched with sadness. "I think about them all the time and wonder what I could've done to change their minds."

"Boots on the ground," Faith cut in. "We need to join the men's discussion, so our team isn't all over the place."

Tony glanced around the cabin. "If you all want to strategize, we need to include Milton and David. He keyed his mike. "Hey, boss. If you have a plan, now might be the time to cue us in. Before we craft one of our own and discover it flies in the face of yours."

Milton's characteristic chuckle blasted through Hope's headsets. "Let me set the PA system so I don't have to keep clicking my mike."

Static crackled, followed by David's voice. He'd been one of Roy's original team members, and was cut from the same mold as all the CIA agents. Tall, rangy, tough as old leather. Only some of them were born with dark hair, but the rest dyed theirs black to blend in with the night they preferred for covert operations.

"Jets just reported." David sounded stoked. "Targets demolished. They're on their way back to Langley."

Muted cheers rose around the cabin, and then Tony held up a

hand, palm outward. "I certainly hope a few freaks are left who'll want to join us."

"Me too, son," Milton said, clearly having heard him. "Our ETA is roughly forty minutes. We'll begin our approach in half that. Eyes on the screen."

A wall screen illuminated on one side of the cabin. After a few flickers, a schematic formed, noting where buildings had been located before the latest jet strafing run. Fortunately, freaks had built their compounds in very out of the way places, so collateral damage to cities, people, and structures was minimal.

"Here," Milton said, and an X formed to the north of the compound. "And here—" another X "—will be where we set down, assuming we can. The first spot will be our bird, the second Roy's."

A ragged, vertical line formed down the center of the schematic. "My game plan is simple. We stick to our side of the compound. Roy and his team take the other one. Keep your kinetics—and your weapons—at the ready. If anyone gives you cause to not trust them, secure them. Use lethal force if indicated."

"Do we have a plan for the women, sir?" Glory asked.

"Same as last time," Milton replied. "If we find women who want to join us, sign them up, but do a damn good job checking their minds—and their motives. Just because someone is female doesn't necessarily mean she won't betray us."

Hope thought about the seven women in her dorm and their deep distrust for Glory. Insofar as they were concerned, she'd left the compound—after killing a Nameless One—which made her and her intentions suspect. Hell, Hope had gone through the tortures of the damned before throwing her lot in with Glory. They'd had to make their minds up fast that night, which hadn't helped.

Or maybe it had. That was one instance where it was good she hadn't had hours to mull her decision. If she had, she might have lost her nerve and stayed put.

"Just did a calculation of winds aloft," David cut in over the intercom. "We're about ten minutes ahead of schedule."

"Excellent," Milton said. "Questions, anyone?"

"What about the Cortexiphan?" Tony asked.

"Glad you asked. You're in charge of hunting for it, in conjunction with Frank."

"If it's us—" Tony sounded dour "—we don't need that fancy ass chemical Geiger counter. It weighs a ton, and we can sense the drug with kinetics."

"More than sense it," another of the Nameless Ones cut in. "It's got a draw that's damn near irresistible. That's why folk like Tony here kept it under lock and key with security devices our kinetics couldn't defeat."

"Is that so?" Milton sounded intrigued. "Why didn't any of you mention that aspect before?"

Hope was watching Tony, and she saw his face redden and his hands ball into fists. "Yeah, it's true. Frank and I decided to keep that part to ourselves for two reasons. We didn't want to admit weakness, mainly, but we also didn't want to plant a seed for those of you who've had the injections. Curiosity's a big draw, and we didn't want a bunch of you experimenting with that drug. Not with its severe side effect profile for normal humans."

He inhaled sharply. "We've been over this ground, but we had no idea how Cortexiphan would interact with the injections. We wouldn't have dosed you with it if we weren't flat out of options."

"You don't need to wonder any longer," Milton said dryly. "I admit it was a rough ride, but I didn't turn into a sunken-eyed addict."

"No, sir, you didn't," Tony agreed, but he didn't sound convinced.

"What aren't you saying?" Hope sent in carefully shielded mind speech.

"He's not out of the woods for a while. You keep that to yourself," Tony cautioned.

Hope nodded.

"What was that about?" Glory asked.

"Something different. Tony was concerned about him and Frank being assigned to a sub-mission without adequate time to plan."

The lie rankled—and Glory probably sensed the falsehood—but worry about Milton ran deep enough for Hope to honor Tony's request. Milton was the main reason freaks were welcome in the CIA. If something happened to him, the odds of them remaining sank to something under fifty percent.

"Contact in twenty," rang in her headset, and Hope girded herself for another day on the field. Being a soldier was hard, but being one step up from a slave in the compounds had been worse.

Much worse.

If they got booted from the CIA, she'd never go back to a compound. She'd die first.

CHAPTER 9

Charlie rested his palm on the cyclic. They'd be at their target very soon. For most of the trip, he'd focused on planning for the upcoming mission. They'd activated the helicopter's noisy intercom system and engaged everyone in a group discussion. Or as Roy called them: group gropes.

Frank had been less than pleased to discover he and Tony would be assigned to locating the drug. His point—and it was a solid one— was that if the two of them were going to be a team, they should've flown together so they could strategize. Roy had come up with something placating about Frank and Tony having so many miles under their belts, they probably didn't even have to talk much anymore. Surprisingly, Frank agreed, and that had been the end of it.

Whenever Charlie wasn't engrossed in details that read like algorithms—if A happens, we do B. If C happens, we do X—his mind turned to Hope. He hadn't slept well, mostly because it took all his self-control not to return to her apartment and pick up where they'd left off. With her in his arms and his mouth glued to hers.

Seeing her on the flight line this morning made him want to run to her and hug her, but he hadn't wanted to make her uncomfortable or create any kind of grist for the gossip mill. Relationships came and went between agents, and he vowed this wouldn't be just one more flash in the pan sexual fling.

No. This was the real thing, and he didn't want any of the men giving him a hard time or seeing her as an easy target. She wasn't. She was his, goddammit. *His.* Maybe he could find out where that hideaway in the San Juan Islands was and make reservations for just the two of them. It was run by a couple of retired agents who understood the value of privacy. Charlie had never wanted to bring anyone there before, but now he did.

"McClaren!" Roy's voice held a sharp edge.

Charlie's head snapped up. "Yeah? Sorry."

Roy narrowed his eyes. "What's gotten into you? I said your name twice before you finally heard me." Charlie opened his mouth, but before he could get any words out, Roy went on. "Is something bothering you? If it is, now would be the time to get it out on the table. We'll be in the thick of things soon, and I need you at a hundred ten percent, not mooning over God knows what."

"I'm good."

"I've known you for a long time. You sure about that?" Roy skewered him with astute blue eyes.

"Double damn sure." Charlie reached across the narrow aisle between the pilot and copilot seats and punched Roy's upper arm. "Let's do this."

So we can get back to Langley, and I can take Hope to dinner like I promised.

"What the hell," Roy muttered. "I tried."

Charlie could've picked up the gambit, but he didn't. He'd told Milton. It was enough. For now. Last thing he needed was a Dutch uncle lecture from Roy, who had indeed been there and done that. Not that he wouldn't tell Roy eventually. He'd tell the world. Scream it from the rooftops, but the message he wanted to broadcast was that Hope would be his wife, and that felt a shred premature. He might have had his eye on her for months, but they'd only agreed to date less than twenty-four hours ago.

A whole lot of water could flow under that bridge. Things might go well, but years of relationship failures dogged him. He'd have to take things slow and be careful not to fall into the same trap where he threw walls up—and his partner told him he was emotionally distant, cold, and unavailable.

Right before she slammed out the door.

"You've got that look again, buddy," Roy observed. "Whatever's eating you, bury it now."

Charlie snapped off an approximation of a salute. "Sir."

Roy rolled his eyes. "Your bird. I'm going in the back to check on everyone's gear."

"Hang on." Charlie tapped a corner of the heads up display. "Put her down here, right?"

"At least you were paying attention to that part. Yeah. Be sure to—"

Charlie made a chopping motion with one hand. "I have hundreds more hours in this craft than you do. You do not need to tell me how to fly."

Roy made a grunting sound. "Touché. Get her on the ground, and we'll launch our part in this." He slipped sideways through the cockpit door.

Charlie heard him talking with the others and turned his attention to the instruments. He fed landing coordinates into the flight computer and let the bird do most of the work. Updrafts from the many smoking buildings below buffeted the craft, but it had enough heft to handle them.

He sent his mind power, augmented by the injection series, zinging outward as he sought freaks who might not have fled after the jets' strafing run. He hadn't expected to find any life below, but if he was reading energy correctly, the compound was crawling with life.

What the hell?

He keyed his mike. "Frank, get up here."

The Nameless One ducked into the cockpit. "Yeah?" He swayed with the motion of the craft as it descended.

"I sense a whole lot of your kin down there."

"Me too. So what?"

"So it means they didn't run away after we bombed the place."

Frank nailed him with his unsettling amber eyes. "Where exactly would you want them to go? It's not as if they have enough vehicles to pile into and leave, and we don't blend in very well. Especially not the men. We scare the crap out of normal humans when we take our dark glasses off, and they're damn hard to justify this time of year. Who wears shades in winter weather?"

"How many do we face once we land?"

Frank frowned. "Between sixty and eighty by my count."

"Does Roy know?"

Frank nodded. "Yeah. I told him. Doesn't change anything except we come out with guns blazing. At least you do."

"Not you?"

Frank cracked a grim smile. "Kinetics, all the way. Never warmed to this—" he patted the automatic rifle slung across his shoulder "—even though you force me to carry it."

"Thanks." Charlie glanced at the other man. "We're landing in about two minutes, you might want to sit somewhere."

"FAA regulations state—"

Charlie chuckled. "You would have the rulebook memorized."

"Yup. All of them. Roy coming back up here?"

"I don't think so."

Frank dropped into the pilot's seat and perched on its edge. Leaning forward, he scanned the ground. "I've been looking. Haven't seen any signs of anyone moving around, which means they have to be in the underground tunnels."

"Makes sense. Those excavations remind me of bomb shelters. When we hit the compound in that Louisiana swamp, everyone scattered. Why not here?"

"Not as many lived at the Louisiana compound, and they had boats and vehicles. No women. Also no subterranean rooms to take cover in. Another issue was that the swamp was inhospitable. Without all their tricks to keep the alligators and cottonmouths at bay—tricks that diverted kinetic energy they suddenly needed to defend themselves—leaving was their only option."

Charlie angled toward an empty spot and dropped the bird into it, cutting the engine as soon as the skids kissed the ground. The main door creaked and groaned as it opened, and Roy's shouts of, "Go, go, go," reverberated off the bird's aluminum walls.

Frank bolted out of his seat. "Just heard from Tony. He's on the ground too, and we have a meeting spot."

"Report on your progress every quarter hour." Charlie unhooked his seat harness and stood.

"Got it." Frank left.

Charlie slid into his field rucksack and tossed his AK-47 over one shoulder. He double checked his ammo clips and snapped on a helmet. Last out of the bird, he somersaulted into a crouch and eyed potential areas where he wouldn't be quite so exposed. Frank had said the other bird was here, which meant Hope was hunting for women to add to their ranks. He wasn't much on religion, but he sent up a quick prayer she wouldn't be subjected to another dorm full of bodies.

The characteristic stench of cordite and expended explosives hung heavy in the winter air. He was grateful for his thick fight suit and gloves. It wasn't much more than ten degrees this morning, but at least it wasn't snowing.

He sent out quick kinetic blasts to locate everyone. They'd disappeared hella fast, or maybe he'd been laggardly leaving the chopper. Usually, he suited up before landing, not after. Roy's energy burned from fifty yards away. The women had found each other, their five unique kinetic fields merged into one another in a shifting kaleidoscope of colors. They'd take care of each other. They'd been doing it for years.

Charlie zigzagged his way to Roy. "Where do you want me?" he asked.

"We could use an extra man in the tunnels. Milton took a team down there. Since no freaks mobbed us after we landed, it has to be where they're hiding. Nearest entrance is about twenty yards north northwest of our position."

An explosion shook the ground, followed by another. Breath hissed through Charlie's teeth. "How many of us went underground?"

"All the men on Milton and David's team except Tony. Gals are combing the ruins for other women."

"Yup. Already located them."

Two more blasts turned the earth under Charlie's boots to a rocking, roiling challenge. He balanced from foot to foot, riding it out.

Roy's wrist computer crackled with Milton's voice. "Kincaid, report."

"Charlie and I are clear. Are you trapped?"

"Not sure. Couple of those fuckers were manning the mainframe. It's how they set off that series of charges that just detonated. They won't be a problem anymore, but I need to figure out if there's an alternate way out of this maze."

"How many are with you?" Charlie asked, wanting to take stock of where everyone was. He kicked himself for not being faster off the blocks getting clear of the chopper.

"Seven," Milton replied, "including two freaks who are working on pulling data out of the computer. They're hunting for schematics since I checked the location where I found an escape hatch last time, and it was a dead end."

"Means six more men and the women are topside," Roy muttered into the microphone. "Should be enough to dig you out if you can't find a back door."

"You're not thinking, Kincaid. Cranes would have a hell of a time with this one. There's not a nice, long, reinforced tunnel like you found in Glory's compound. I'll let you know what happens."

Roy signed off and exchanged a pointed glance with Charlie. "Air won't be great down there. Not for very long."

"Those central computer dens of theirs must be well-ventilated," Charlie argued. "Or else there'd be no way to draw off the heat they produce."

"Good point, so long as explosions didn't block the ductwork. Let's locate who we have to work with up here. By my count, it's Frank, Tony, two of the newer freak recruits, and a couple of us old-timers. And the women."

Charlie felt more than heard an alteration in the air currents. "Watch out!" he shrieked and pivoted sideways. The freak who'd been headed right toward him, pitched onto his knees, but he was fast. Before Charlie could congratulate himself on a move well-played, the Nameless One launched himself at him, focusing kinetics meant to fry his brain.

Charlie angled the side of his hand, chopping hard into the freak's neck. It had the desired effect. His eyes rolled upward until mostly whites showed, and he slumped to the ground unconscious. Charlie sprinted to where Roy rolled on the ground, locked in combat with another freak. Slotting his arms beneath the man's biceps, Charlie yanked his arms behind him in a karate lock.

The freak writhed in Charlie's grip, and Roy slithered out from beneath him. He pulled a nasty-looking knife—with an eight-inch, serrated blade—from a sheath and held it to the freak's throat. Roy broke the skin for emphasis, and crimson drops scattered, rich with the copper stench of blood.

"Where's the back entrance for the mainframe's room?" Charlie growled next to the man's ear.

"Why the fuck should I tell you? You're just going to kill me."

"Not necessarily." Roy's voice was smooth, good cop to Charlie's bad one, despite the knife he held at the freak's throat. "Did you see our amnesty offer?"

"Pfft." The man twisted his head and spat on the ground. "Tricks. More tricks."

"No. Several of you work for us, and we'd welcome more. We're not murderers, and you have skills we can put to good use," Roy replied.

"Women!" shrilled in Charlie's head. *"We found lots of women. Alive!"*

"Hope? That you?"

"No. It's me, Glory. Instructions, please. We tried to raise Milton, but all we got was a bunch of static."

"Is he okay?" another voice, presumably Honor, cut in.

"Alive, but buried with the mainframe. Seems to be one of his new tricks," Roy replied, sounding dour. Clearly he was recalling another raid where Milton ended up trapped underground with another mainframe.

"I get it," the freak Charlie still held in a death grip, muttered. "Your leader is the one trapped. It's why you asked about a way out."

"We'd do that for any of our men—or women," Roy replied. "We don't assign different values to life based on rank."

"What do we do with them?" Glory asked again.

"How many are there?" Roy cut in, having clearly been privy to the telepathic exchange.

"Ten who are willing to take a chance on freedom," Honor said.

"How many who'd just as soon knife us in the back?" Charlie asked, and held his breath. The ones rejecting amnesty shouldn't be allowed to live, but he didn't have it in him to order the women to execute their own.

"Twelve. This is Hope, Charlie. Maybe if we brought them back too, they'd change their minds after a while. They're in the same place the seven women in our dorm were the night you rescued us. They don't know whom to trust, and they're scared."

"You hear that?" Charlie angled his gaze at Roy.

"Yeah. It brings up a whole shitpile of problems. Like how the fuck will we transport a dozen reluctant recruits who could join their kinetics and sabotage the helicopters? Not sure our chaff could keep that many out at close range."

"We could hit up the nearest field office to send vehicles." Charlie hunted for solutions. The pain in Hope's voice had been palpable. Not only could they not order her or any of her sisters to terminate the twelve who didn't want to sign on, it would be hard to justify killing them outright absent full-on treason.

"Ha!" The freak, who'd stopped struggling against Charlie's martial arts hold, spat on the ground again. "Better send an armored car if you want to corral those bitches."

"A way out of the tunnel system," Roy pressed.

"What's in it for me?" The freak turned his amber eyes with their vertical slit pupils Roy's way.

"You could sign on with us." Charlie mirrored Roy's earlier suggestion. "Decide now. It's not as if you have a whole lot of options. Either you're with us, or you're on the run heading for another compound. Those eyes of yours are impossible to conceal, so the odds of you blending in anywhere are nil."

"What are you going to do with the women who told you to piss off?" the man countered.

"We haven't figured that out yet. Once we do, it's none of your affair," Charlie replied.

The man he'd nailed moaned from where he lay sprawled on the ground. Roy bounded to him, brandishing his knife. "Awake enough to talk?"

"Mmph." The man started to sit.

"Not so fast. You're flat on the ground until we figure some things out."

"Like what? If you're going to kill me, get it over with." The freak's voice was muffled since he lay face down.

"You could work for us. Beats being dead," Roy observed dryly.

"Huh?" The freak turned his head so he faced Roy. "I heard about that amnesty offer but figured it was a bogus myth. No one here believed it."

"It's real, but you need to decide which horse you're riding. We've got bigger problems right now."

"Permission to sit, uh, sir."

"No. I like it better with you right where you are. Do you know where the escape route out of your mainframe room is?"

"Of course. It's—"

"Shut up!" the other freak screeched. "I'm negotiating over here."

"Can't find shit," Milton's voice, partially obliterated by static, crackled through Roy's wrist computer. "Smoke's getting thick down here. Can't figure out where it's coming from so we can block it. Or at least slow it down."

"Casualties?" Roy asked.

"Not yet. Maybe another half hour before the air's too toxic to breathe."

The crackling stopped. Roy looked from one freak to the other. "If there's a way into your underground hellhole besides the main passageway, tell me now. That man down there is like a father to me. You won't give a shit about that part, but he's a friend to your kind. It's because of him and his intercession that freaks have a place in the CIA. A whole lot of agents disagreed with him for accepting you, but he held fast. He even took injections to make him more like you, despite the docs telling him he was too old."

"Yeah, he damn near died because of them," Charlie cut in. "But he still supports freaks integrating with the rest of us. He's married to one of you and Roy here is married to another."

The first man's amber eyes widened. "You took our women?"

"They came willingly," Roy snarled. "The night I met Glory, she was half-frozen, more than half-starved, and I've never seen a woman quite so scared." He stalked back to the man Charlie still hung onto and shook his shoulders. "You did that to her. Not you personally, but others just like you. I should hate you for what you did to the woman I love, but I've found a way to live with it."

"You fucked us over first," the freak pointed out.

"It doesn't matter," Charlie said. "No one can change the past.

Not us, and not you with your augmented mental power. Now is there a back way out of the tunnels, or shall we all start digging?"

The freak sagged in Charlie's grip. "Let go and I'll take you. You can follow me. If I don't deliver, I'm fully expecting a bullet in the back of my head."

"Nah," Charlie said. "If you fuck us, I'll turn you around so I can see the light go out of your eyes after I've carved you up a little." He let go of the freak. "Hurry."

"I want to come," the freak on the ground cried. "I know where it is too."

"Fine. Get up and get moving," Roy gritted out.

The men took off at such a quick pace, matching it taxed Charlie. Fuck the fancy genetics that had gone into making these guys. He'd give anything if the injections had made him even more like the specimens racing in front of him.

Who wouldn't want to be Superman?

Roy panted from behind, running hard to keep up.

The first freak skidded to a stop over a patch of dirt that looked like every other patch of dirt for a hundred-yard radius. "Here." He dropped to his knees and scrabbled at the dirt with his fingers curved into claws. The second freak did the same, moving dirt aside.

"Do you need us to help?" Charlie asked.

"No." The sound of fingernails scraping metal replaced the nails on rock and dirt sound, and a metal ring came into view.

Charlie crouched and cleared dirt away from the rough outline of a door. "Where exactly does this go?" he asked.

"The computer room. Where else?" The second freak rocked back on his heels. "If that's where they're trapped, this goes to a panel concealed in the back wall. You can find it from the inside, but you have to know exactly where to look. It blends in with the rock."

"You go first." Roy prodded him in the back with his rifle butt.

"Oh ye of little faith," the first freak smirked.

"Yeah, forgive me for not suspecting you'd wait till me and

Charlie were in the tunnel, and then you'd shut and latch this door. Not my first rodeo, dude."

"I had no idea you normies were so funny." The freak almost cracked a smile and pulled the gateway open, dropping into the hole.

The second freak jumped in after him.

"Charlie!" Glory's voice reminded him he'd never gotten back to her about the women.

Roy had already entered the gaping pit, following the freaks. Charlie could've conferred with him. Instead, he made a field decision. *"Bring all of them with us. Assign the willing ones to watch over the unwilling ones, and hope to hell it will be enough to get all of us back to Langley in one piece."*

"Thank you." Hope's voice rang with relief. *"You won't be sorry. I'll see to it."*

Charlie scanned the area before following the other three down a ladder.

"Charlie!" Frank sounded just as stressed as everyone else, but he never sounded overly chipper about much of anything. Maybe he was just reporting in as ordered.

"Yeah. What's up?"

"We located the Cortexiphan, but we could use a spot of help."

Charlie stared down the hole. Leaving Roy by himself with two freaks didn't feel like a huge risk. He keyed his wrist computer. "Roy. Something's might've come up. You good down there without me?"

"You're kidding, right? I'm behind them with a drawn gun. Is it the women?"

"No. They're fine. It's Frank and Tony."

"They find the shit?"

Charlie breathed a little easier when Roy didn't spell out the name of the drug. It might be like waving a cooked spoon of heroin in front of addicts for all he knew. "Yes, but there's a problem."

"Find out what it is and fix it. Once Milton and the others are free, we can get out of here."

"On it."

Charlie turned his attention back to Frank. *"Specify type of help needed."*

"As many agents as possible. Most of the freaks are in a bunker on the western edge of the compound. It escaped destruction. The drug is there too, but Tony and I don't have a death wish."

"Two against fifty isn't good enough odds, huh?" Charlie joked.

"More like eighty-three," Tony cut in. *"Figure something out. They know we're out here."*

"Drop back," Charlie said. *"That's an order. I don't want them commandeering you back into their ranks."*

He moved away from the opening in the earth and got his bearings, using kinetics to determine his position and everyone else's. He didn't want to use telepathy to craft plans, not when freaks could listen in.

"To me," he sent. *"Priority one. Now."*

CHAPTER 10

*H*ope was hustling women into one of the helicopters when she intercepted Charlie's orders. She looked from Glory to Honor since they were closest. "Sounds urgent."

"Can we help?" one of the women who'd jumped on the amnesty bargain offered, her green eyes shining with enthusiasm.

"I want to help too," another woman chimed in. "Being freed was awesome, but if we could strike a blow against the Nameless Ones too—"

"—it would be even better." The first woman finished her sentence.

Hope knew exactly how they felt. She'd been there. Steeped in hatred for the men who pushed them around and choreographed their every move, while rationing essentials from food to bedding.

"I don't know how I feel about your CIA," one of the other women muttered, "but I hate all the Nameless Ones."

"Yeah, if the CIA didn't have men, it would be a big improvement," another said.

Hope laughed. "Not all of them are like Nameless Ones."

"But a whole bunch of them come close," Honor cautioned. "Pays to be careful, no matter which world you live in."

"We need to get moving," Glory spoke up. "Double time. Now. Who's in?"

"What if we don't go with you?" A woman who hadn't said much moved to the front of the group. Her dark hair was woven into many braids, and her green eyes were narrowed to suspicious slits.

"You can wait for us here," Glory said. "Or this would be an excellent opportunity for you to run, but I've been there. Life in the compound isn't any kind of preparation for life on the road. Think about your choices. It's not smart to jettison something you don't understand in favor of a second thing you don't understand, either."

Glory took off, running fast without looking back. She didn't have to. She'd shared her wisdom and the women would either listen—or not.

Hope pelted after her, avoiding the temptation to look behind her or use kinetics to judge how many women had joined them. She wanted to save them all, but it wasn't realistic. Driven by fear and years of poor treatment, some of the women would fade into the surrounding countryside.

She sent her ability outward seeking Charlie's exact location. His energy pulsed warmly, and she longed to stand by his side. Even if they were comrades in arms today, rather than lovers, being next to him filled her with anticipation. His revelation from the previous night still seemed impossible, but she hadn't imagined it.

Honor and Glory found normal men to love them. No reason the magic can't work for me too.

She reached Charlie right after Glory and Honor, who were peppering him with questions.

He held up a hand. "Wait until everyone is here. Otherwise I'll cover the same ground over and over."

"Who's everyone?" Honor demanded. "Do you know where Milton is?"

"Yeah. He's underground with the mainframe that runs this place, but explosions rendered his original route inoperative. Roy and some freaks who knew an alternate route out of there are on their way to spring him."

Honor squared her shoulders. "I want to go. You said underground, so that fresh hole I passed on my way here must be the route inside." She started back the other way.

"Honor. Remain here," Charlie barked. "No room for more personnel in that tunnel, plus Roy isn't expecting you—or anyone else—to block the exit route."

"But—" Honor spun to face him, mulish determination stamped into her features.

"No buts. Get your ass front and center now." Charlie sounded every inch the commander he was, his years of military experience apparent and his usual laissez-faire attitude nowhere in sight.

Women joined them. Hope counted heads. Elation ran strong, lightening her spirit. All but two were part of the circle growing around Charlie.

He scanned the group. "Is this it for women?" he asked Glory.

"Seems so," she replied. "I gave them choices. The two who are missing either ran, or they're back at the chopper."

Two men who'd been part of Roy's original team trotted up. "We've been keeping an eye on the perimeter," one said. "Deactivated a couple men we caught running away. Where do you need us?"

Charlie gestured for them to close in. "Not sure which is safer, but since I'm not any good at shielding my telepathy, I'm going with keeping my voice low. Frank and Tony need us. They located the bulk of the residents of this compound—and the drug."

"Uh, yeah. The bunker on the west side of these grounds, right?" one of the new women looked pointedly at Charlie.

He stared back. "If I want input, I'll ask for it. Otherwise, hold your questions."

She skinned her lips back from her teeth and poked Faith. "How is he any different from the Nameless Ones?"

"Ssht," Faith hissed. "You're free to leave if you think you can do better elsewhere."

"Enough." Charlie made a chopping motion with one hand.

"What's the plan once we get to the bunker?" one of the men asked. Jet-black hair fell into his dark eyes, and he was dressed in the same, dark insulated flight suit that was CIA regulation issue.

"Depends." Charlie raked his gaze over the assembled women. "You gals ready to fight?"

"Never readier." One stepped forward and folded her arms beneath her breasts.

"Excellent. It means you follow orders, though. We can't have ten different battle plans."

"Got it. Don't mind Emma over there." She pointed at the woman who'd bitched about Charlie being a stand-in for the freak men.

A feral grin spread across Charlie's face. "So long as you lend your kinetics, I'll overlook a whole lot. You just might make the difference here. I hadn't counted on twenty more on our side." He rattled off a string of coordinates. "We'll finalize strategy once we get there. Let's go."

"What I don't get is why no one's fighting us," one of the women muttered.

"Cause the cowards all went to ground to save their own precious hides," Hope replied. "If you want to be part of this mission, get moving." She dialed in the compass that lived in her brain and headed for Charlie's coordinates.

He fell into step next to her. "Good to see you."

She glanced his way. "Same here. I'm not supposed to indulge in emotions, but I was thrilled to find two dorms full of women. Live women."

"If they're anything like you, they'll be a treasure."

"Aw, thank you." Her face grew warm, so she ran harder to avoid the temptation to throw her arms around him.

"Charlie!" Frank's stage whisper drew her to a precipitous halt, and she skidded on an icy patch of dirt as she changed direction.

"You moved," Charlie noted from where he stood nose to nose with Frank and Tony.

"You told us to fall back." Tony sounded testy.

A metal globe landed with a *thud* between them. "Fuck!" Tony scooped it up and heaved it hard. A blast wave hit Hope, followed by two more, and she struggled to remain upright.

"What the hell?" She shook herself. "Where's the noise? It must've exploded. Why couldn't I hear anything?"

"It's a grenade," Frank said, as if that explained it.

"An ultrasonic one." Charlie grabbed another out of the air and chucked it.

This time, Hope was ready for the effect and hunkered low, bracing herself. "How long have they been throwing these?" she asked.

"Started right before you got here," Tony said.

"They only have a few." One of the new women spoke up.

"How do you know?" Frank demanded.

"Because I helped make them. How else?" The woman sounded annoyed. "If you alter the chemical composition, you get almost the same stopping power, but they're silent, so they're easier to use in crowded places like supply houses. People get confused, and—"

"You can tell us later," Charlie broke in. "We're separating into four teams. Leaders are Charity, Tony, Glory, and me. Teams one and two will circle around the back. Teams three and four will hit from the sides. Find a way in. Once you're there, kill on sight. Use kinetics if you can. If not, watch the potential ricochet pattern for bullets."

"Really?" one of the new women squealed. "We can kill Nameless Ones?"

Charlie nailed her with a grim look. "Normally, we'd offer amnesty, but my best guess is the ones holed up in that building would refuse."

"Assuming we can get inside, which is far from a given, what happens after we get the drug?" Tony asked. "Frank and I are on separate teams, but that doubles our odds of locating it."

"What else?" Frank laughed. "We run like hell."

"The rest of us will leave too," Charlie said. "We're not killing any more freaks than is absolutely necessary."

"We'll let you know once we're clear—if we find it." Tony gave a thumbs-up sign.

"Same on my end," Frank agreed.

"You be fucking careful." Charity moved to Tony's side and gave him a quick, hard hug.

"Always. You too, sweetheart. We should be proud. Charlie trusted each of us with our own team."

"We can be proud afterward. Right now it's premature."

"My fierce warrior. It's okay to let yourself feel good about—"

"Not before we achieve a desirable outcome," Charity insisted, and Hope could've hugged her. Charity had struggled with an unstable genome that nearly killed her, but she'd come through stronger and more irascible than ever.

Honor sidled next to Hope and switched to shielded telepathy. *"I'm worried about Milton. If it was as simple as one of the tunnels going to the computer mainframe, he'd be out by now."*

"How do you know he isn't?" Hope infused optimism she wasn't feeling into her question.

"I'd sense him, and I don't." She bent close. *"I'm going back to where I saw that trap door in the ground. If Charlie notices, cover for me. Tell him I went to pee or something."*

Before Hope could dissuade her, the other woman slipped away, using the crowd to conceal her movements. Hope watched her sidelong, admiring her skill. Honor had always been gutsy, but the CIA had trained her well, adding to her abilities.

Charlie was assigning them to groups. His motives were suspect, but she was glad to end up with him. Faith, Frank, and two of the new women were also in their group, and they worked their way the last quarter mile to the rear of a concrete block building half sunk into the ground. No windows. No visible way in beyond a single door in front.

Hope stared at it. Tony's words echoed in her mind. *Assuming we can get inside, which is far from a given.* So this was what he'd meant.

Nothing like this existed at her home compound. It had to be something new, developed as a result of the war that had escalated after she and the other four women defected. At least there hadn't been any more of the weird grenades. The ones that blasted you with ultrasonic waves that didn't touch the hearing spectrum.

"There has to be more than a single entrance," Charlie muttered, taking in the squat structure.

"There is, but it's underground," one of the new women said. "The Nameless Ones added to the tunnel system."

"Shit!" Frank raked a hand through his unkempt, dark hair. "If we'd known that, we'd have been better off going with Milton."

"Wrong," Charlie said. "Milton's trapped down there."

"Just because he is doesn't mean I'd be." Frank sounded smug. Vintage Nameless One. Hope resisted an urge to slap him.

Charlie tapped his wrist computer. "Listen up, everyone. Does anyone see a way inside?"

"Front door is it," Tony said. "That was my assessment earlier too. Want to gather the groups and storm the fortress? My team is ready."

"It's not a sound move," Charlie muttered. "Kind of like the Germans at Stalingrad."

"Huh? Gotta look that one up."

"Doesn't matter. To borrow a page from your book, our odds of everyone surviving aren't good. If we blast the door and race through once it explodes, they'll be laying for us inside. It's what I'd do under the same circumstances. They could pick us off one by one as we enter the building. We'd kill a bunch of them, but they'd kill more of us."

"I could walk up to the door and knock," one of the women suggested. "The Nameless Ones have no idea I switched sides."

"No go." Charlie shook his head. "You're on my team now. You might get the door open, but as soon as they figured out you lied, they'd kill you."

"What are you thinking?" Frank asked.

"That you can synthesize the drug. This mission just got way more complicated than any of us expected. Extricating Milton and Roy are my top priority. Once we have them, I say we take the freaks who want to defect and get the hell out of here."

"You're the boss," Frank muttered, "but it's a mistake to leave any stores of Cortexiphan. Freaks can use it to make themselves invincible—at least until it destroys them. Meantime, they could inflict a whole bunch of damage none of us can predict."

"Fine. We'll send the jets back. They can finish what they should've done earlier today," Charlie retorted. "I don't recall this bunker being part of any of the schematics I studied, which is why they missed it.

Hope felt for him. No easy answers, but he'd prioritized his people over the drug, and she respected him for that.

An explosion rocked the ground beneath her and made her ears ache. This was their grenades, not the ultrasonic ones. More blasts buffeted her. Charlie drove her to the ground with his body atop hers, cursing.

"Report," he barked, presumably into his wrist computer. "Who attacked the bunker without my authorization?"

"Not my team," Glory's voice broke up through the wrist computer's tinny speaker.

"Not mine," Tony and Charity said almost in unison.

A loud cracking noise ripped through Hope. Its metal grating against metal quality made her teeth hurt. The stench of cordite and gunpowder thickened the cold air, burning her lungs and eyes. "Whatever it is just tore the door off its hinges," she told Charlie.

"Yeah, I figured that out." He rolled off her and bent over his wrist computer. "To the front of this fucker. Now. Make sure whom you're targeting. Do not use lethal force unless you see your opponent. Wait until they exit to subdue them."

How could our grenades have gotten inside?

The answer slammed through Hope, obvious in its simplicity. Roy had found his way to Milton, but instead of leaving the underground maze, they'd punched through to beneath the bunker. Maybe the two newly recruited Nameless Ones had spilled enough beans to alert Milton the only way he'd gain the upper hand would be from beneath.

She slid into a crouch where she crab walked around the building, zigging from side to side to lessen the odds of one of the freaks getting a bead on her with kinetics. Shrieks and cries blasted from the front of the building. Tears streaked her face from her stinging eyes as more smoke filled the air.

"Outside now if you want to live," Milton's voice boomed.

Hope straightened and bolted around the corner. Damn if she hadn't nailed this one. Milton, a very much alive Milton with soot streaked down his face and Honor by his side, herded freaks through the front door. He chivied his group off to one side away from the door, which suggested the building was far from empty.

"I don't fucking think so," Roy roared, just before a blast of automatic weapon fire added still more stench and smoke to the winter morning. Bodies rolled through the door spewing blood. High, thin cries gave way to silence. The acrid smells of blood, shit, and vomit mingled with all the other noxious scents of battle. Roy marched ten freaks with their hands held behind their heads out the door.

"Anyone else feel like throwing their life away?" Charlie queried in a grim, don't-fuck-with-us tone, and helped Roy move his group of freaks toward the ones standing with Milton and Honor.

Frank ducked through the open doorway, heading into the bunker. Apparently, he'd decided it was time to hunt down the drug.

"Watch yourself," Roy called after him. "Not sure we got everyone."

"Charity! Join my team with yours," Tony yelled and bolted after Frank.

Hope gritted her teeth together so hard, she was surprised they didn't shatter from the pressure. She willed Frank and Tony to find the drug fast, so they could leave before anyone else had to die today. She'd hated the Nameless Ones, but it didn't mean death was any kind of comfort zone.

One man who wasn't quite dead, but would be soon judging from the gaping hole in his gut and intestines spilling into the dirt, moaned piteously. Hope focused a band of kinetics to stop his heart.

She glanced around the clearing. Who the hell could she trust? Lots of freaks had integrated into the CIA with few problems, but that was a while back. Was there a new master plan to defect and then sabotage from within? Back when she'd lived in a compound, the Nameless Ones had a plan they constantly fine-tuned. The bottom line was they wanted payback for the original breeding farms. No one ever said, "To hell with it, we need to let it go and move on."

No. Revenge was where they lived. Hope was certain that part hadn't changed.

A flash of kinetics blasted through the front door that had been ripped from its hinges. "Down!" she shrieked and hit the dirt on her belly.

A blast of machine gun fire was followed by unholy wailing, and three bodies fell through the doorway, riddled with bullets. Hope tested the area around the bunker for freak power, but she couldn't sort friend from foe. Her ears rang from the blast, and when she pushed to her hands and knees, taking stock of the damage, she couldn't find Charlie.

Where was he?

She lurched to her feet, where she'd have a better vantage point, and saw him, sprawled face down in the icy dirt with Milton crouched next to him. "Stay with me, son," Milton muttered. "You are not allowed to die."

Blood fanned in a pool from beneath Charlie's body. An icy wave of fear cascaded through her. All she saw were rivulets of red, and Charlie's life draining from him. Hope had no idea how she got to Charlie, but she plowed into Milton, pushing him aside. "Need to turn him over. Got to see what we're dealing with here."

"He might have a spinal cord injury," Milton protested, grabbing her hands.

"If he dies from blood loss," she cried yanking her fingers from his grip, "it won't matter which part of him is injured."

"Shit!" Faith hovered over her. "Let me help. I worked with medical sometimes."

"Get Frank and Tony." Hope kept her gaze glued on Charlie, willing the damage not to be as bad as she feared.

"Even better. I'm on it." Faith sprinted for the bunker shrieking both men's names.

Hope reached beneath Charlie and turned him so she could see the places kinetics had blasted him. They'd missed his heart. She knew that before she turned him. If his heart had taken a direct hit, it would have exploded inside his chest. That was the problem with kinetic wounds: small entrance holes and maximum tissue and organ damage, not unlike hollow point shells.

Where was all the blood coming from? It seeped through his skin from internal injuries. She put pressure on the places the epidermis seemed weakest. Tears mingled with the smoke stinging her eyes.

"Can you tell what's damaged?" Milton's voice, low and desperate, vibrated next to her.

"No. Goddammit." She moved her red-stained hands to a new spot where blood oozed through ruptured skin cells.

Frank skidded to her side and dropped to his knees. "Jesus." He ran his hands up and down Charlie's body, seeking information. "Was he the only one injured?"

"No. One of the women from this compound went down too," Milton said, tightlipped. "She's right over— What the holy hell? She's not there anymore?"

"I'm all right," a woman croaked from somewhere behind them. "Wasn't as bad for me, but my physiology is different."

Tony joined them, kneeling in the ice-crusted mud. He dragged a black bag open and extracted a syringe and a glass ampoule. "Move aside," he grunted. "This might do it."

"I'm not through assessing the damage," Frank protested.

"Ruptured liver and spleen. Probably pancreas too," Tony said. "If he were one of us, he'd survive just like that woman did. The injections didn't confer enough of our cellular recuperative powers, though. New cells can't regenerate fast enough to replace the damaged ones. Meanwhile, he's bleeding to death internally. It's not the same as when we dosed you—" he angled a momentary glance Milton's way "—but the principles are the same. Without Cortexiphan, his odds of survival are zero."

"We could call an ambulance, have him transported to a level one trauma center," Milton argued. "Cortexiphan is a risk."

"A necessary one," Tony argued. "His insides are scrambled."

"He'd die en route to any hospital, even if one was across the road from this compound," Frank said, his voice devoid of inflection.

"What are the odds?" Hope asked.

"Certain death without Cortexiphan," Tony said. "Fifty-fifty with it, assuming its side effects don't kill or cripple him."

Hope fought to swallow around a golf-ball sized lump in her throat. She wanted to throw her body across Charlie's, protect him from what might end up being worse than death, but dissolving into hysterics would sign his death warrant.

Honor crouched next to her and wrapped an arm around her shoulders. "You have to believe it will work out. I sat with Milton through the same thing."

Hope couldn't talk, so she leaned into her friend, grateful for her solid presence.

Tony drew the straw-colored drug into a syringe. "Frank. Find me a vein."

"I can do that." Hope dragged a knife from a thigh sheath and ripped a long hole down one arm of Charlie's flight suit.

Frank pushed fabric out of the way and pressed the flat of his hand across Charlie's lower bicep. Vessels barely showed, and Hope's heart sank. He'd lost so much blood, they were too late. She sank to the ground next to him and wound her arms around him, careful to stay out of Frank and Tony's way.

Honor kept an arm around her, adjusting her position.

"You cannot die," Hope whispered into his ear. "We just found each other. Hang on for me. For us."

"Got one," Tony said. "Hang onto him. Gonna be a rough ride when the drug hits."

"I have his legs," Frank said.

Milton pushed Hope aside, but not very much. "Stay on top of that shoulder," he instructed in a surprisingly gentle voice. "I have the other one. We want to make sure he doesn't break any bones and make things worse."

"Will this work?" Hope tried for steady, but her voice cracked and broke.

"Won't know for a while," Frank said. "Hang on. Here it comes. Tony just took the needle out."

Moments ticked by, and nothing happened. Hope searched with kinetics and felt Charlie's life force, but it was faint, so faint she checked again to make certain she wasn't mistaken.

The shift from comatose to frenetic movement happened fast. Charlie's body stiffened against her hold on him. His back arched like a bow, and he bellowed in pain. His feet drummed against the dirt, and he cried out again.

"Frank. Do something," Hope pleaded.

"We did all we can," Frank replied. "What happens next is up to Charlie."

"Can't you give him something to cut the pain?" she asked.

"If we do, we'll kill him for sure," Tony said.

"I made it through this," Milton said. "Charlie's tougher than me. Hell, this time tomorrow night, we'll be sharing shots of whiskey and one upping each other."

Hope kept a kinetic thread latched into Charlie. At least he was still alive. Barely. *"Live,"* she urged in shielded telepathy. *"Do not let the bastards steal you from me."*

She wasn't certain of much of anything, but if Charlie died, she'd turn into a one-woman show, intent on taking down every single compound and every single Nameless One. She'd kill until they took her out, and she couldn't kill anymore.

End of story.

CHAPTER 11

Charlie felt the kinetic barrage before it hit him. Displacement in the air currents tipped him off, but he wasn't fast enough pivoting out of the line of fire. He heard shouting and the rattle of automatic rifles. He tried to hoist his weapon, but his body wouldn't cooperate. That was his first clue he'd been hit. There wasn't any pain, just a crippling inertia. He sent his augmented senses inward, assessing damage. He hadn't expected to find much, but when the extent of his internal injuries registered, shock set in. No one could live with his liver, spleen and pancreas shredded. He had to be bleeding like a gutted pig. If his lungs weren't filling with blood, they soon would be.

A downward glance just before he crumpled into the dirt showed blood—his blood—spewing from multiple spots. It didn't compute. There weren't holes in his body there, but blood oozed through anyway. Had whatever hit him damaged his skin? Weakened it?

He tried diverting his enhanced abilities to the injured place with stern instructions to repair the damage, but nothing happened. Was he too far gone? Or had the injections not conferred enough of the freaks' inherent regenerative ability?

Hope.

Where was she? Had she been hit too? He tried twisting his neck, but his body rejected his brain's directions. He opened his mouth, tried to call her, but no sound emerged. He'd entered an odd type of Hell, one where he was still sentient, but incapable of communicating.

Fuck! I can't do anything but lie here, dying.

The thought was harsh, sobering, and true.

Charlie felt himself sinking, felt darkness close over him. He fought against the sensation, but cold seeped upward, chilling his bones. Part of him was tired, wanted to give up. There were worse ways to die. Ways that hurt a whole hell of a lot more than what had happened to him.

No! an inner voice screamed.

I have to live. I never told Hope how much she means to me. We have a life to live. If I check out now, it'll never happen.

Milton grabbed his shoulder. Charlie wanted to reassure his commander he was okay, but he couldn't turn his head or open his eyes.

"Stay with me, son," Milton urged. "You are not allowed to die."

Hope materialized next. Thank fucking God she was alive and uninjured. "Need to turn him over," she told Milton. "Got to see what we're dealing with here."

"He might have a spinal cord injury," Milton protested.

"If he dies from blood loss," she cried "it won't matter which part of him is injured."

Charlie wanted to roll over and draw her into his arms, but not so much as an eyelash worked the way he wanted. He'd seen enough death on the world's battlefields, he knew his body was shutting down.

Please, he pleaded with God, if there was such a thing. *Let me tell her I love her.*

But God wasn't in a cooperative mood.

"Shit!" Faith's voice buzzed next to his ear. "Let me help. I worked with medical sometimes."

"Get Frank and Tony," Hope yelled.

"Even better. I'm on it." Faith shrieked both men's names to the accompaniment of her scurrying footsteps.

Hope reached beneath him and turned him onto his back. He didn't feel the movement, but light brightened behind his closed lids. And pressure points shifted.

"Can you tell what's damaged?" Milton's voice, low and desperate.

"No. Goddammit."

Frank skidded to Charlie's side and dropped to his knees. "Jesus!" He ran his hands up and down Charlie's body, seeking information, except Charlie scarcely felt the freak touching him. Words flowed around him, but they mingled into a confusing mélange.

Tony joined them. "Move aside," he grunted. "This might do it." He must be on the ground like everyone else. At least Charlie heard him. He tried again to open his eyes, but nothing happened.

"I'm not through assessing the damage," Frank protested.

"Ruptured liver and spleen. Probably pancreas too," Tony said. "If he were one of us, he'd survive just like that woman did."

Woman? What woman? It was a minor point, but Charlie was afraid if he let go of even the smallest detail, his life would slip away, maybe without him even noticing.

Tony was still talking, but Charlie had missed the first part. "… enough of our cellular recuperative powers. New cells can't regenerate fast enough to replace the damaged ones. Meanwhile, he's bleeding to death internally. Without Cortexiphan, his odds of survival are zero."

"We could call an ambulance, have him transported to a level one trauma center," Milton argued. "Cortexiphan is a risk."

"A necessary one," Tony argued. "His insides are scrambled."

"He'd die en route to any hospital, even if one was across the road from this compound," Frank said, his voice devoid of inflection.

"What are the odds?" Hope asked.

"Certain death without Cortexiphan," Tony replied. "Fifty-fifty with it, assuming its side effects don't kill or cripple him."

Certain death, certain death hit Charlie like a sledgehammer.

It's not as if I didn't know.

Yeah, but hearing it ain't easy.

"Frank. Find me a vein," Tony said.

"I can do that." Hope must've drawn her knife because something ripped a long hole down one arm of his flight suit.

Frank pressed the flat of his hand across Charlie's lower bicep on a hunt for a vein.

Cortexiphan. If Charlie had anything left, he'd have felt afraid. Odds for humans injected with the drug weren't good. He could go mad. End up drooling and in diapers. It wasn't any kind of life. He tried to open his mouth, to scream he'd rather be dead than a blithering idiot, but nothing came out.

Big surprise. Words haven't been there since this fucker started.

"You cannot die," Hope whispered into his ear. "We just found each other. Hang on for me. For us."

He ached to reply. To tell her he'd try his best, but he couldn't even let her know he'd heard her.

"Got one," Tony said. "Hang onto him. Gonna be a rough ride when the drug hits."

The needle bit and stung as Tony injected Cortexiphan into him.

"I have his legs," Frank said.

"Stay on top of that shoulder," Milton instructed in a surprisingly gentle voice. "I have the other one. We want to make sure he doesn't break any bones and make things worse."

"Will this work?" Hope's voice cracked and broke.

"Won't know for a while," Frank said. "Hang on. Here it comes. Tony just took the needle out."

The shift from comatose to frenetic movement happened fast.

His body stiffened against everyone's hold on him. His back arched like a bow, and he bellowed in pain. His feet drummed against the dirt, and he cried out again. White-hot heat poured through him, burning every nerve ending to cinders. Maybe he'd died after all, and this was what Hell was like.

"Frank. Do something," Hope pleaded.

Hope. If I can hear her, then I'm not in Hell.

Another wave of agony ripped through him, obliterating both words and thoughts.

"We did all we can," Frank replied. "What happens next is up to Charlie."

"Can't you give him something to cut the pain?" Hope asked.

"If we do, we'll kill him for sure," Tony said.

"I made it through this," Milton said. "Charlie's tougher than me. Hell, this time tomorrow night, we'll be sharing shots of whiskey and one upping each other."

Misery dogged him, groundswell after groundswell of knives carving flesh from his bones. At least he could feel something again, but he longed for surcease from the escalating pain. He cursed himself for being a coward, did what he could to gird himself against the next onslaught, but they were unpredictable. One minute his guts burned with a fury, the next it felt like someone was sawing his feet off at the ankles. His fingers felt like they were burning, only to regenerate so they could burn once more. His back bowed again of its own accord, almost as if he were stretched across the racks that were a staple item in medieval torture chambers.

Milton went through this.

So fucking what? We've always said he was too tough to die.

Yeah, well I am too.

Charlie wanted it to be true, but curling up into an agonized ball trumped everything. He heard the wounded animal sounds coming from his throat, but when he tried to stem them, it did no good. He fought multiple sets of hands holding him down, but they were stronger than he was. Even if he'd been free, he didn't have any idea what he'd do with himself.

The knives switched focus, attacking his brain. The worst headache imaginable throbbed everywhere at once until he longed for unconsciousness, but refused to give in. If he did, death hovered within easy reach. He'd be goddamned if he'd offer himself up to the Grim Reaper like a giftwrapped roast.

"Don't fight it." Frank gripped his head between impossibly strong hands. "Let go. When you wake up, the worst of the pain will be gone."

"Who would've thought he'd be this strong?" Tony's voice vibrated like a gong that had been struck one too many times.

"He's scared," Hope said. "Scared if he passes out, he'll never wake up."

Charlie forced his eyes open, focusing on her face with gargantuan effort. "Not scared," he panted. Not—" Darkness hit him with all the force of a tsunami, dragging him into the void.

THE VIBRATION of rotors hauled Charlie back to consciousness. He was in a chopper. He recognized the thrum of the Chinook's powerful pistons keeping them airborne. Could he still open his eyes? The last thing he'd seen was Hope's worried face. He scrunched his lids experimentally, mostly to see if his motor control had returned or whether it remained elusive.

Someone leaned over him. "Stay quiet," Frank said. "You're strapped to a backboard. It'll feel claustrophobic as hell if you start thrashing around."

"Been there. Done that." Charlie's voice emerged as a whispery croak, but at least he had one. Even better, it responded when his brain told it to. He opened dry, sandpapery eyes and saw Frank straighten above him.

"He's awake," Hope cried, followed by the clatter of her seat harness as she unclipped and joined him where his litter was attached to the floor.

"You should be in your seat," Frank noted.

"So should you," she retorted and pushed hair out of Charlie's face. "How are you feeling?"

"Like a train ran over me. Thirsty."

Hope started to get up, but Frank closed a hand over her arm. "No water. Not yet. And especially not with him flat on his back."

"Sorry," Hope mumbled. "Wasn't thinking about that part."

Charlie focused on Frank. It took way more effort than it should have to marshal his thoughts and trade them for words. "This forty something percent side effect gig from Cortexiphan. What do they look like? How long until—?"

Frank held up a hand cutting off Charlie's halting flow of words. "The second question is easier. If you make it through the first couple months, you'll likely be fine. The drug hasn't been used in enough humans for me to tell you what the side effects will be with any level of certainty, let alone how they might impact you."

"Yeah, but they stopped clinical trials with it for a reason," Charlie pressed. "What was it?"

"Not an *it*. Several problems cropped up, all manifesting at higher than acceptable levels. Mental instability, marked by excessive aggression was the primary one. Early dementia another. Amnesia ran a close third, except it never lifted."

"Milton was fine," Hope argued.

Frank nailed her with a pointed look. "Milton is fine now. Got to wait out the clock on him."

Hope pressed her lips into a thin line, but didn't say anything else.

"How long till we land?" Charlie asked. After he got back, there'd be time to read up on the things that might happen. Or not. He hadn't had a choice. Frank and Tony had saved his life. Now it was up to him to keep his ship on course. Just like always.

Since the dye was cast, and there was no going back, he might be better off not dissecting every single emotion, worrying if it was a harbinger of volatility.

"Maybe half an hour," Hope replied. "You were out for most of the trip. Aw shit! I was supposed to let Milton know as soon as you came around."

"I'll do that," Frank said and got to his feet. "Could use a bit of a stretch."

"Guess we traded who was in which bird." Charlie met Hope's direct gaze.

"We did. Milton wanted to be in control of the craft that took you back to Langley. Roy's his copilot. You should've heard him ordering the flight crews at Bangor International around while they refueled us. They've probably never run so fast. I'm sure it was a relief when we left."

Charlie smiled weakly. "Yeah, Milton can be a real bastard when people don't move quick enough to suit him. Who's flying the other bird? I'm certified in this craft. So's David, but that's about it. Is he flying without a copilot?"

"Of course not. Tony's helping."

Charlie would've shaken his head, except it was pinned in place by a plastic collar. "You guys don't need to be certified, huh?"

"Nah, we just establish a link with the computer. Machinery likes us." She smiled, and his heart melted. "We ended up with a bunch of potential recruits from this mission. Twenty women and half that number of Nameless Ones."

"Gotta be careful," Charlie began, and then shut up. He didn't want to hurt her feelings by implying the freaks might have less than stellar motives. After what happened to him outside the bunker, though, it was harder than fuck to trust them.

A cacophony of opinions ripped through his head. The one that rose to the fore informed him Hope was a *them*, and if he couldn't trust freaks, he couldn't trust her, either. He told it to shut up.

"Are you feeling worse?" Hope bent closer, concern spilling from her green eyes.

"Headache. It'll pass." He did not plan to tell her about hearing voices. Auditory hallucinations, to put a finer point on them. Not with the specter of Cortexiphan hanging over him.

"I hope so. Back to the recruits, we are taking all precautions. Milton already told them they'd be on probation and limited to certain areas of the campus until they've proven themselves." Hope rattled on, oblivious to Charlie's concerns about putting his foot in his mouth or the unwanted voices that had yet to shut up. "I'm thrilled we finally have more women, and that—"

"You're awake!" Milton boomed and settled to the floor on the other side of Charlie's litter. "Can you move everything? I argued against this backboard, but Roy insisted. He's the one with paramedic training, so I capitulated, but so long as…"

"He stays where he is." Roy's voice crackled over the intercom system. "Until we're back at Langley and medical clears him."

"Damn! Busted." Milton glanced at the speaker mounted on one wall. He squeezed Charlie's shoulder. "Glad to see you up and about. I'm still experimenting with improvements since I had the Cortexiphan, but I think you'll be pleased."

"Landing in nine minutes," Roy told everyone. "Strap in now."

"See you on the ground," Milton said and stood, trotting back toward the cockpit.

"You should be in your seat." Charlie wanted to reach for Hope, but he was swathed in a blanket and strapped to a board. Nothing was free, not his hands, not his feet. Maybe it was just as well. He didn't want to make her uncomfortable with a public display of affection. He had no idea if she'd mentioned him to Glory or Honor or Faith or Charity.

"Yeah, but I'd rather be here," she said.

Frank entered Charlie's limited line of vision. "Into your seat for landing." He placed his hands under Hope's arms and hauled her upright.

"Let go of me." She twisted in Frank's grip, but he held firm.

"As soon as you promise me you'll strap in. Roy wants everyone in their seats for landing."

"Leave her alone," Charlie shouted, and then felt like an idiot.

"I didn't hurt her," Frank protested.

Anger pummeled Charlie. He wanted to haul off and punch Frank for laying hands on Hope. Powerless took on a whole new aspect from his prone position, and he fought to hang onto the cool, collected center that had seen him through war zones and times when action wasn't prudent.

He could punch Frank later.

How about not punching him at all?

A deeply irrational part wasn't buying it, though. Frank had touched Hope. Not okay. She was his woman. *His.* Any other man who got close to her needed his balls shoved up his ass.

Jesus! Chill. What the fuck is wrong with me?

Hope retreated to her seat, grumbling. Frank moved to a place Charlie couldn't see him. The collar that was part of the backboard kept him from turning his head.

Breathe, he instructed himself, still grappling with fury that refused to recede.

Pressure changes in his ears told him they were almost there just before the skids kissed the ground.

Hope was out of her seat and by his side fast. "I have to help the new women settle in. I'll check on you later in the infirmary." After a gentle pat on his shoulder, she left at a quick clip.

Outrage swelled. He should be her first priority. To hell with the new recruits. Let someone else show them to their quarters. Before he could open his mouth to inform Hope her place was by his side, she was gone.

Charlie sucked air like a bellows. Not fighting the restraints became a fulltime job. Even tougher was not focusing his kinetics to spring himself. A crew of four paramedics he'd never seen before knelt by his litter and unhooked it from the helicopter's floor.

"You good, dude?" One of the men shoved his face inches from Charlie's.

Charlie skinned his lips back from his teeth. "No. Get me out of this straightjacket now. That's an order, soldier."

"Sure, sir. Whatever you say, sir." The medic smiled benignly.

Charlie recognized the tactic. It was designed to smooth things over, avoid arguments with irascible patients. Except that wasn't him. He was fine. Just fine. The rest of the world needed an attitude adjustment.

"Tell us how you were injured, sir," another of the paramedics spoke up.

"Freak kinetics."

"You need to say more than that, sir." The first man nodded sharply, and Charlie's litter lifted from its resting place as they carried him from the chopper, angling the litter to get him through the door and down the steps.

Anger, apparently his new go-to place, bubbled hot. He wanted to scream at the medics to unstrap him. He'd go to his quarters, goddammit, not the infirmary. That was a place for sick people. He wasn't sick. He just needed a few hours' sleep, and he'd be right as rain again.

"Let me go." He infused authority into the command.

"Of course, sir," the first medic said without even looking at him.

"Just as soon as Doc Thomas gives us leave," the second medic said. "Decisions like that are above our pay grade."

Charlie drew on the reservoir that held his power. It responded fast, much faster than it ever had before. Had to be the Cortexiphan potentiating whatever the injections had altered.

The four medics slid his litter into the back of a waiting van, locking it into place. "We'll have you at the infirmary in less than three minutes, sir," the first medic said, smiling brightly.

"You're in good hands," another of them piped up. "No better place to bring battlefield injuries than Doc Thomas. He served in the Middle East and—"

"Shut the fuck up," Charlie screamed. "I served with him. When he finds out you refused a direct order from me, he'll have you court-martialed."

"Yes, sir." Medic one sounded far too cheerful. The van doors slammed and it took off at far more than Langley's posted thirty mile per hour speed.

"Pistols at dawn," Charlie shrieked, his head pounding mercilessly.

"Certainly, sir. Except I'd rather we used sabers. I used to fence on the Olympic team," the medic replied. Settling next to Charlie, he slithered two fingers inside the neck brace, right over his carotid.

"How is he?" one of the medics asked from somewhere in the front of the vehicle.

"Pulse one fifty. Weak. Thready. Pupils dilated. Hurry. Call the doc, and have him meet us outside with something to knock Special Agent McClaren out."

"No. No more drugs," Charlie shouted, but it was hard to catch his breath. Something was sitting on his chest, weighting his lungs. The harder he tried to suck air deep into them, the more elusive breathing became.

Darkness circled again. Somewhere in its velvet depths, he could've sworn he saw a figure in robes laughing his head off.

CHAPTER 12

Hope made her way across Langley's grounds under a gray sky spitting sleet. It was late afternoon, but she'd been in contact with the nurse assigned to Charlie throughout the day. He'd had some kind of seizure in the transport vehicle and had lost consciousness again. Since there wasn't much point mooning over his bed and getting in the way of people providing for his care, she'd spent the past few hours making certain the new women were comfortable and knew where to find what they needed on the sprawling Langley campus.

They'd been so pathetically grateful, it tore a hole in her heart. She remembered her own raw gratitude the first time she'd seen not just a pallet, but an entire apartment that was all hers. And food. More food than anyone could possibly consume, lined up on serving tables in the cafeteria. Reliving the miracle had been humbling, and she vowed never to take anything in her new life for granted.

"Wait up," sounded from behind her.

She turned at the sound of Tony's voice. Frank loped next to him. Both men wore grim expressions that were easy enough to read.

Hope tilted her chin upward. "Charlie's still alive," she said defiantly. "At least he was two minutes ago. What's wrong?"

"We need to talk," Frank grated. "Privately, where no one is likely to overhear."

"Which rules out the infirmary," Tony broke in. "That is where you were headed, right?"

She nodded mutely, not trusting her voice.

"Let's use one of the basement rooms in Milton's building." Frank changed direction without waiting to hear her assent.

It was such a Nameless One move, it made her blood boil, but if anyone held the key to fixing what was going on with Charlie, it was Frank and Tony. Talented geneticists, they'd trained themselves, which meant they weren't bound by any kind of traditional science.

"True enough," Tony said, "and yeah, I was inside your head. Before you hand me a raft of grief for violating your boundaries, these are critical times that justify it. Frank told me you're interested in Charlie. Presumably, he shares that interest. You could be a pivotal—"

"Shut up," Frank hissed. He yanked a side door open after tripping the lock with kinetics and herded them inside.

The downstairs corridor was lit with recessed fluorescent bulbs. Frank twisted the knob on the first door they came to. It opened onto a small classroom, lined with tables and chairs. "This'll do," he said and shut the door, locking it behind them.

Tony pulled the shades on windows lining one wall and dragged three chairs into a rough circle.

Hope got the picture. She dropped into one of the chairs. "What's wrong with him?" she demanded. "Milton got better. Why is Charlie getting worse?"

"If we knew, it would be easier to fix," Frank said. Breath whistled through his teeth. "Charlie had the original batch of injections. He and Roy were the only ones who got that exact configuration, and it was rough. They were sick with gut cramps and muscle aches for a couple months."

"By the time the rest of Roy's team and Milton took the series—" Tony jumped into the conversation "—the CIA scientists had refined the mixture. Made it easier on human physiology."

"So we have two sets of variables that are interacting differently in two human subjects," Frank said.

"Actually three," Tony muttered.

"Three? What's the third?" Hope chewed her lower lip. Without waiting for an answer, she blurted, "Was the Cortexiphan different too? Maybe synthesized with slightly divergent chemicals because it was all this batch of freaks could get their hands on?"

Frank furled his brows. "Gotta hand it to you, woman. You're sharp. That's exactly what Tony and I have been doing. Testing the two batches, and yeah, there are some salient differences." He hesitated. "If we'd known, we might not have been so fast to inject Charlie."

"Yeah, we would've," Tony corrected. "The man was dying. Our backs were against the wall. Again. At least that part worked. He's alive."

Hope shook her head. "He's not going to want to just be alive. If he loses all the things he loves, turns into someone he can't respect, that's probably worse for him than being dead."

"We know that," Frank said. "In addition to performing chemical analysis on the two types of Cortexiphan, we did a few other experiments." He leveled his odd eyes on her. "Did you sleep with him?"

Heat rose from her neck to the top of her head, and she shrugged her hood back to deflect the warmth. "No. Why'd you ask?"

"Damn." Tony fisted a hand and pounded it into the other one. "We were hoping we could use some of your blood to create an antidote. Something to encourage his human parts—and push back the machine aspects."

"Did you ever wonder why we're on V4 for our genome?" Frank asked, the question seemingly rising out of nowhere.

"Because the first three were unstable," she said.

"Unstable is a kind word," Tony snarled. "V2 imploded. They caught fire. Burned from the inside out. No way to save them other than killing them."

"Yeah, I remember that," Hope said. "It was only the men, but that was before you turned into Nameless Ones. It was also the final straw, the thing that spawned our rebellion where we blew up the breeding farms."

"Right." Frank narrowed his eyes to slits. "V3 was our own fix. We came up with it, not the humans. It wasn't perfect, but at least it didn't kill us. Not many of us, anyway. V4 was—"

"What does this have to do with Charlie?" She spoke over him, anxious to get to the infirmary. If it truly was hopeless, she wanted to spend Charlie's last hours with him. Maybe he'd have a lucid moment before he died. If that happened—

Tony made a chopping motion with one hand. "You've watched too many soap operas or read too many romance novels. None of this 'sit by his bedside wringing your hands' crap, sister. We need your help."

"Fine." She snapped off the word. "Tell me what I can do."

He drew a syringe from a black briefcase he'd carried into the room. "Clear a vein. I need your blood. Even though you two didn't actually have sex, it still might work."

Hope considered asking what he was going to do with her blood, but she kept her mouth shut and stripped off her hooded jacket. Next came her thick outer top. When she was down to long underwear, she rolled up a sleeve, baring her forearm.

Tony put pressure just above the bend in her arm, inserted the needle, and waited while her blood filled the syringe. Meantime, Frank spread some items on a table. When Tony was done, he handed her blood over, and Frank proceeded to split the contents of the syringe among four test tubes.

Hope applied pressure over the needle hole with a piece of gauze. "What are you doing?" She stood and walked to where Frank was dripping various chemicals into the tubes, and then testing them with litmus paper. Some tubes received drops of additional chemicals predicated on the outcome.

"Several things," he replied without looking up. "This first test station tells me just how different your blood—and hence your genome—is from ours. Tony and I have almost identical genomes. Back before we even dosed Milton, we ascertained we couldn't have helped him if the Cortexiphan destroyed his brain's ability to keep the limbic system under cortical control."

"Limbic. That's emotion, right?" Hope asked.

"Yeah," Tony answered. "The other chemical tests Frank is running are predicated on a positive outcome for the first. We had Honor as an ace in the hole for Milton. Turned out we didn't need her."

Hope tugged her sleeve down and slipped into her other tops to stay warm. The room had a heater, but turning on much of anything might alert security to their presence, and the fewer who knew about their impromptu meeting, the better.

"Did Honor know that?"

"No," Frank replied. "And you're not going to tell her, either."

"Okay. I won't tell her. Why'd you ask if we'd had sex? If it would help, I can figure out how to chase everyone out of his room, and—"

"It's not the physical act so much as the emotional bonding. Once you have sex with someone, there are subtle alterations in the paleo mammalian cortex, also known as the limbic system," Tony explained. "That feeling of being in love has physical and chemical markers that match up. If your relationship had become physical, they'd be far better defined."

"We're hoping to identify and use those markers in an infusion to fix the parts in his central nervous system that are degrading," Frank said. "Bodies are nothing but constellations of chemical and electrical impulses. We can manipulate most of them, so long as we get in there before there's too much damage."

"Degrading? I don't like the sound of that." Hope wrapped her arms around herself. Despite not being outside, she suppressed a shiver. "In lay language, what's happening to him?"

"Best we can tell, the neuronal pathways feeding his cortex—that's his higher reasoning ability, the part that makes him Charlie—are being diverted in favor of more reptilian brain function. It doesn't help that the paleo mammalian cortex has all but shut down."

Hope had requested the information, but it still felt like Frank had sucker-punched her in the gut. "Can you fix it?" she asked.

"We don't know," Tony replied. "Uncharted territory. We've never done anything like this before. We have stained slides of his cells, though, and a CAT scan of his brain. I believe one of the docs ordered an MRI. Once it comes through, we'll nab that too. It's clear enough what needs to change to salvage him. We just have to figure out how to make it happen. Which combo of chemical and electrolyte markers will reverse the damage."

"I'm surprised the MDs cooperated to the extent of sharing lab results," Hope muttered.

"They didn't." Frank muffled a grunt. "Anything in Langley's computer banks is fair game, though."

"The tricky part will be sneaking in there to dose him and hanging around to see what effect our efforts have," Tony muttered. "If the medical personnel chase us out, we might not be there at a critical juncture."

"True enough." Frank bent over his test tubes, shining an ultraviolet light on them. "So much of this is trial and error. We have to be there to see what to change—if our first shot out of the box doesn't do it, or makes things worse."

"Have you gotten Milton involved?" Hope demanded.

"Not yet," Tony replied. "Remember, he's not exactly out of the woods from his own Cortexiphan experiment. We didn't want to stress him unduly right now."

Almost as if talking about Milton drew him, the door to their classroom opened inward, rattling against its stops, and he strode inside, kicking the door shut behind him.

"Report!" he barked. "Medical informed me someone hacked into McClaren's computerized records. It has to be the two of you. I want to hear everything, and I want to hear it now."

"Take it." Frank jerked his chin at Tony. "I'm busy here. Since we've been discovered, turn the lights on."

"Here goes," Tony said. "As soon as we heard about Charlie's escalating aggression, we knew we'd have to intervene…"

Milton listened, inserting questions at intervals. "Are there more than two versions of Cortexiphan?" he asked when Tony stopped talking.

"We weren't aware there was more than one until earlier today," Tony answered. "Like I said at the front end of this, when Charlie started to demonstrate increasing instability, we got to work."

"Why didn't you solicit my help?" Milton sounded gruff. "That way you wouldn't have had to sneak data out of the computers."

Frank straightened from where he'd been bent over whatever experiment he was running. "Is that really important?"

"No. What'd you find over there?" Milton gestured toward the constellation of test tubes.

"Hope has enough common markers with Charlie, it might work to prep an infusion using her serum."

"Will that retard damage from the Cortexiphan?" Milton asked.

Hope kept her eyes riveted to Frank. For good measure, she dug into his mind, willing him to tell the truth. Nameless Ones were notorious for hedging, when it was in their best interest. It wasn't that Frank didn't care what happened to Charlie, but he loved science first and foremost. This was as juicy a project as he'd probably run across in a long time. Lots of variables and a phalanx of unknowns.

"I don't know for sure," Frank admitted. "If it works, it'll do more than slow the damage, it'll reverse it."

"How long will it take to prep the infusion?" Milton glanced from Tony to Frank.

"We have the base in these last two tubes," Frank said. "Maybe an hour. I need to get back to my lab."

"Use the one in the hospital," Milton said. "Your lab is clear across Langley's grounds." He tapped keys on his wrist computer and barked a few orders.

Hope heard someone protesting on the other end, complaining about non-MDs having access to a man whose vitals were unstable. Milton told him to stuff it and signed off. He trained his dark eyes on Frank and Tony. "Do not let Charlie die. If the shit you give him kills him—or turns him into a vegetable—I'll catch God's own grief from Doc Thomas. That man has a long memory, and he can be relentless."

"We'll do our best." Frank's amber eyes shone with enthusiasm. He carefully gathered his mini-science experiment, stoppering the tubes and then tucking them into holders in the black briefcase and clipping it shut.

"Ready?" Tony sounded almost as excited as Frank looked.

"You will not discuss this with anyone," Milton cautioned. "Understand?"

"Got it," Frank followed Tony out the door and into the darkened hallway beyond.

Hope started after them.

"Not so fast," Milton ordered.

"Sir?" Hope swung to face him. "I want to go to the infirmary. Even if Charlie isn't conscious, maybe something I say will sink in. Hearing is the last sense to go. Even unconscious people—"

"Stand down. I'm not stopping you. All I'll take is a moment or two of your time. The night before our last mission, Charlie told me you were important to him. I wanted to make certain you have feelings for him too. He and I go back a long way. All my men are like family to me. Hell, they were my only family until I found Honor."

Milton's forthright nature might have bothered a normal human, but Hope found it comforting. It fit with her lack of subterfuge and her tendency to call a spade a spade.

She squared her shoulders and faced Milton. "Yes, he's important to me. We'd decided to...get to know each other better." Hope squeezed her eyes shut for a moment. When she opened them, she said, "He can't die, sir. We won't let him."

"That's the spirit." Milton clapped her on the shoulder. "Get moving. I'll meet you at the infirmary. Those MDs need a firm hand. They get uppity sometimes."

Hope beat back half a smile. Milton was impossible not to like. "Thank you, sir." She trotted out the door.

"Just doing what I need to do to keep this place running," he called after her.

Hope pushed the door open and ran hard, headed for the infirmary. Milton's reactions tonight went a long way toward helping her see through to the man beneath his commander persona. He felt the same way about the CIA as Frank and Tony did about science. He'd go to the mat to preserve the institution and its agents, and she respected the hell out of him for it.

"Milton told me." Honor's voice rang in her head. *"Would you like me there?"*

The hot, quick bite of tears prickled behind Hope's lids. *"Yes."*

"See you very soon," the other woman said. *"Hang in there, hon. We'll see him through this. No matter what it takes."*

Hope's first problem reared its head when she tried the retinal scanner mounted by the infirmary's main door, and the lock didn't disengage. She could spring it with kinetics, but should she? She didn't want to be on everyone's wrong side the second she showed up in the midst of a bevy of medical personnel who knew she had no right to be there.

She scanned instructions on a plaque bolted next to the door and engaged the intercom, identifying herself and the patient she wanted to visit.

"Sorry," a tinny voice informed her. "Agent McClaren isn't in any shape for visitors."

"Milton Reins is meeting me here," she countered.

"Fine. Have him buzz us when he shows up." The crackle of the intercom went dead.

Honor ran up to her. "What's wrong? Why are you just standing here?"

"They won't let me in."

"Oh really?" Honor pressed the intercom. When no one answered, she jabbed it again.

"They probably think it's me," Hope said.

Honor stared at the lock. It whirred, and buzzed. She shoved the glass door with her hip and mock bowed. "After you."

"Jesus, Honor. They'll be pissed."

"Who cares? We came to see Charlie. Milton will be here soon. He was stopping by to get Roy. Or at least alert him about Charlie going downhill."

Hope followed Honor inside. The fluorescents were so bright she squinted and willed her pupils to constrict. "Tony and Frank must already be here." She pulled the building's schematics out of her database brain. "Lab is on the second floor. Northwest corner."

"Yeah and Charlie is at the opposite end of that floor in their iso rooms," Honor said and headed for a door marked, *Stairs*.

A buxom blonde woman swathed in teal scrubs bustled from one of the hallways. "I didn't buzz you in." She made shooing motions with both hands. "I'm sick of you people busting in here. Go. We'll let you know if there's any change in Agent McClaren's condition."

"You people?" Honor's voice rose with outrage. "Would you care to clarify that statement?"

Hope dragged on her arm. *"Not the time for a confrontation,"* she sent in mind speech.

The blonde's pale cheeks reddened. Before she could formulate a response, Milton's unique energy signature closed from behind

Hope, followed by his heavy tread. "They're here on my authority, Rayna. Return to your station."

She bristled. "Why even have security here if everyone ignores it?"

"We pay you to do a job. Get back to it."

"Yes, sir." She turned on her heel and trudged back the way she'd come.

Milton dragged the stairwell door open. "This way." He motioned. "I was here earlier."

Hope followed him with Honor behind her. The trip up two long flights and down an equally long hall seemed to take forever. Before they got to the end, an outraged bellow rattled her eardrums.

Charlie.

Hope broke into a run, pushing around Milton and past two agents who blocked the door. She'd been ready to blast them with kinetics if they didn't move aside. Maybe Milton had motioned them to stand down. He was behind her, so she couldn't see him.

She burst into the room and stopped cold. Charlie thrashed against wrist and ankle restraints, his face carved into a rictus of agony. She'd expected unconscious—until she heard him shouting. She hadn't anticipated this. He shrieked again, straining against his bonds.

Going to him, cradling him in her arms as she'd planned was out of the question. "Charlie?" She tried to make eye contact, but his rolled crazily.

"Charlie, I'm here." Hope tried again, louder this time, and moved closer to the bed.

His rolling gaze zeroed in on her, but his eyes had the vacant look of a madman. "You got my name right, bitch, but who the hell are you?"

Hope couldn't help herself. She sent kinetics into his mind, searching for the man she'd fought alongside these past few months. His brainwaves crashed together in erratic configurations, neurons firing without pattern or reason.

A grim bleakness settled into the pit of her stomach. They were too late.

No one could claw their way back from the kind of destruction she'd just witnessed. Hope turned toward the door. Charlie was still screaming, but she blocked it out. It wasn't Charlie strapped to that bed. Not anymore.

Milton's face held a horrified expression. He smoothed his features to neutrality, but the message was poignantly clear.

"He's worse, huh?" she asked.

"That's an understatement. I'm headed for the lab. If Frank and Tony don't show up soon with a fix, Charlie will sink so deep into the pit we'll never get him back."

CHAPTER 13

Hope felt Honor's arms close around her and realized she'd shut her eyes to erase everything. Charlie's descent to the Ninth Circle of Hell. Milton's outrage and despair. Everything.

"Be strong," Honor urged.

"I'm trying, but it's really, really hard." Hope let Honor lead her into the hallway past the agents standing guard at the door. They had sidearms. Were their instructions to subdue him with lethal force if it came to it?

Don't be ridiculous. All agents carry weapons. I'm really losing it.

Frank and Tony pelted down the hall, wheeling a small cart between them. Milton strode behind. "Are you sure this will work?" he called after them.

"No." Frank didn't even turn around.

Another low, guttural shriek came from Charlie's room.

"From the sound of things, I give it less than fifty percent," Tony muttered.

"What would improve those odds?" The sound of her voice surprised Hope. She'd thought the question, but apparently it came out her mouth too.

Frank stopped at the door to Charlie's room and twisted to face Hope. "You. You could improve them, but the risk is significant."

"Clarify." Milton stepped between them.

"She joins her mind with his via kinetics and sends her energy to redirect and repair the places that are breaking down."

"I'm not a she." Hope stuck her face right in front of Frank's. "I'm right here, and I just pushed into what's left of his mind with kinetics. It's not pretty, and I haven't got clue one how I could fix the churning mess I found."

"We'd walk you through it," Tony said. "In fact, I'd be right there with you. It's similar to what I did the night we almost lost Charity."

"What about the infusion you prepped?" Milton asked.

"Oh, he'll get that too." Frank narrowed his eyes. "He's deteriorating by the moment. We need to at least get that started." He skewered Hope with his slitted gaze. "Decide fast, sister."

"Want to talk about it?" Honor whispered into her ear.

"Not sure what good talking will do," Hope whispered back. "Either I do it. Or not." She longed to tell Honor that she'd been Frank and Tony's fallback position with Milton, but she'd promised to keep her mouth shut about that. "Thanks for being here."

"Least I can do. We're sisters. We went through hell in that compound, and we stick together."

A tall, thin man in a white lab coat with *Reginald Thomas, MD* blazoned over the left chest pocket trotted up to Milton. Dark hair was shorn close to his head, and his astute green eyes brimmed with annoyance. "I demand to know what you plan to do with my patient. He's dying. His vitals are eroding. Blood pressure and heart rate are too high. Electrolytes are all over the map."

"You tell him," Frank elbowed Tony before pushing the small cart into Charlie's room.

"Why do you want to know?" Tony countered. "The way we view physiology is considerably different from how you were trained."

"He's my patient." Dr. Thomas poked Tony's chest with an index finger. "It's kind of like being pilot in command of an aircraft. Only one of you is in charge at a time. It cleans things up, makes them less confusing. Right now, I'm pilot in command of this patient."

Tony's nostrils flared with irritation. "Keep your hands to yourself. You wouldn't poke me if I were another M.D."

"I need help in here," Frank yelled.

Hope slithered through the group blocking the doorway and ran to him. "What's happening?"

"Charlie pulled his IV out. Need to reset it somewhere he can't get to it and wrap that arm to stop the bleeding. I need this infusion to go in all at once, and I need to do it now, which is impossible with him thrashing around."

"It'll take more than just me to hold him steady for you," Hope muttered.

"What's in that syringe?" Dr. Thomas pushed between them, eyeing the cranberry-colored mixture nested in a heated pod atop the small table.

"A serum reduction with added electrolytes and a calcium channel agent to increase blood and oxygen flow to his heart. I also put in some of the original batch of Cortexiphan to see if it doesn't correct the problems with what I gave him in the field."

"Whose serum? Did you type and crossmatch it? You can't mean the Cortexiphan I think you do," the doctor sputtered. "That drug was dropped from clinical trials. Did you—?"

The restraints creaked alarmingly as Charlie fought them. It was how he'd dislodged his IV, by flailing from side to side.

Milton materialized with the two agents who'd been guarding the door. "Grab him," he instructed tersely.

A hatchet-faced nurse pushed past everyone and went to work on the displaced IV line.

Honor joined Milton. "I'll help. Four is better than three."

"Thanks," Milton replied tersely. "Grab a limb, everyone."

"Give me that." The doctor picked up the syringe and strode to the bed. "Turn his head so I have a clear shot at the jugular." He spared a murderous glance at Frank. "If I inject this and it kills him, I will see you hung by your balls."

"He's going to die anyway if we do nothing," Frank pointed out. "Even you said that out in the hallway."

"Shitcan the threats and the catty observations," Milton snarled. "We're holding him steady. Get that infusion on board."

"I hear and obey, oh fearless leader, but it runs counter to my medical judgement." Dr. Thomas inserted the cannula and began feeding Frank and Tony's concoction into Charlie.

The man was competent and fast. Not surprising since he'd been a field surgeon in the Middle East like… Hope's head snapped up. She'd gleaned that bit of data from her sojourn through Charlie's mind. She must've since she had no other way of knowing it. She'd never heard of Dr. Thomas until showing up in the infirmary.

Maybe Charlie's brain wasn't as jumbled as she feared, if he was thinking about the doctor who was treating him.

Tony joined them, adding to the claustrophobic feel of the already small space. "I'll do it," Hope told him.

"Do what?" Tony's gaze was plastered on the doctor as he injected the infusion.

"The kinetic mind meld."

Tony looked at her then. Really looked at her. "Are you sure? You could go mad. He might drag you into the blackness along with him."

"Could you reprogram me if that happens? Like you did with Charity?"

His stark features softened, and Hope understood why Charity had fallen in love despite him being a Nameless One. "Maybe."

"Odds?"

He shrugged. "Between sixty-three and sixty-seven percent."

"Better than I thought. When do we begin?"

"Give that infusion about ten minutes to go to work after the doc is done injecting it."

"You're in?" Frank sidled next to her.

"Yeah. Tony said ten minutes."

"That's about right." He focused on the monitors. "At least they're moving in the right direction."

"He's not thrashing as much," Hope observed. "At first I thought it was my imagination, but he's not straining against everyone holding him." She looked for the nurse, but the woman had vanished once she'd reestablished the IV tubing and dealt with blood oozing from the original insertion point.

"Pressure and heartrate are down by ten percent." Frank sounded positively jovial, and he fist pumped the air.

"That could change fast," Tony cautioned him. "Might be an artifact of some of the extras we put in the infusion. Things to calm his system enough for the real work to happen."

Hope wanted to understand everything. What changes the injection series had created in Charlie's body. How the Cortexiphan interacted with them. "The damage from the freaks who attacked him earlier," she began, searching for words.

"His damaged organs are repaired, for the most part." Tony intuited what she wanted to know. "The Cortexiphan took care of that, but it created new problems. Those are the ones we're dealing with now."

"The original wounds would've killed him, right?" She searched Tony's face for truth, and found it in his unwavering gaze.

"Of course. Frank and I aren't in the habit of interfering with something that packs an unknown punch if we don't have to. Are you ready?"

Hope focused her mind, pushing the human parts to a less prominent place. She was scared. Her heart was beating fast, and her mouth was dry. Sweat beaded on her forehead and dripped down her sides.

"Yes."

"Listen carefully. Focus a small kinetic beam at a point right here." He tapped his head just behind one ear. "I'll join my mind with yours. Imagine our kinetics as strands wrapped around each other. Once we're inside, let me guide where we go."

"It's a real mess in there," she muttered.

"If it's so bad repair is out of the question, we'll withdraw. No point in chancing this if the odds are stacked against us."

"Why will I risk madness and you don't?"

"Your genome is configured differently than mine, and now it's linked to Charlie through the infusion. That makes you more susceptible to him sucking you into the hell he's mucking around in."

"So it would've been safer for me if you hadn't given him whatever was in that syringe?"

"Somewhat. Maybe a few percentage points, but it wasn't negotiable. He had to have the infusion."

"Look sharp, both of you. It's time," Frank said.

"Can I help?" Honor asked.

"No. Too many cooks," Frank replied.

"Good thing," Milton growled low. "I love you for volunteering, Honor, but I do not want you in jeopardy."

"Love you too, but I make those decisions for myself." Honor touched Hope's shoulder. "Let me know if you need more juice. I'll be right here."

Hope moved next to the bed. Charlie appeared unconscious, his face an ashen gray and his breathing shallow. It was an improvement from him struggling against the leather pieces binding him to the bedframe, but he was still dying. No one could remain that color for long and live.

She took a few steadying breaths and honed a beam of kinetic power, keeping it modest like Tony suggested. She aimed it behind Charlie's ear and felt Tony's kinetics join hers. Last time, she'd careened deep very fast. Now she took her time, using the extension of her mind to examine one layer of brain material at a time.

Charlie flinched beneath their invasion. *"Are we hurting him?"* she asked Tony.

"No, but he'll be aware of us soon."

"What happens then?"

"We'll find out together." Tony moved closer to her, and for once in her life, she was grateful for a Nameless One's solid presence. *"Call him,"* Tony suggested. *"Just his name. Get him used to you being joined with him."*

"Charlie. It's Hope."

The tangled mass of neurons in front of her kinetic beam might have quivered slightly. She wasn't certain, so she called his name again. This time, a definite opening formed, rather like a dark funnel. If it wasn't an invitation, she'd never seen one, so she pushed into it, hoping to hell it wasn't a trap. Charlie was a well-trained commando. Surely something as simplistic as setting and springing a snare for an enemy would be second nature.

I'm not his enemy.

Maybe not, but last time he didn't even recognize me.

"Focus." Tony breathed the word into her mind. *"Keep going. Say his name again."*

"Charlie. You need to come back."

"Can't. I've tried."

Hope swallowed back tears. He sounded like himself. It had to be a good sign. *"You have to. No choice."*

"Every time I try, it sucks me under. Hurts so bad. Easier this way."

"You have to fight this. If you don't, the life you love pitting yourself against danger won't be there anymore. Beyond that, you and I can't ever be together."

He was silent for so long, she wondered if she'd lost him and pushed in a little farther.

"You're here. You could stay." His mind voice sounded different this time. Cagey, devious, laden with conspiracy. *"If you wanted to."* A hesitation. *"It would be better for me if you were here."*

Movement out of the corner of her eye caught her attention. When she looked at Tony, he was shaking his head emphatically and mouthing the word no.

Hope licked dry lips. *"The place you are. It's not a place I can stay for long."*

"Why not?"

"It will suck the life out of me, and then the woman you held in your arms the other night won't exist anymore."

"But we'd be together," he insisted.

"Not the right way. Come on, Charlie. Fight this. You're strong. It's one of the reasons I want to be with you."

"There's no way out. I've tried. It's good now. You're with me, and the pain is gone. Please stay, Hope."

His words pierced her heart, even while the wrongness in his logic jarred her.

She focused her mind voice for Tony. *"What do we do now?"*

Except Charlie heard her. *"Who are you talking to?"* he demanded.

"It's Tony. Hope's talking with me. I'm here with her, and we're both trying to help you find a way back because she loves you, and—"

"She's mine," Charlie yelled. *"You leave her alone."*

"Of course she's yours. Charity is my woman, remember? I pulled her back from the abyss just like I'm trying to rescue you—if you'll let me."

Hope glanced at Tony, but he held up a hand telling her to wait.

Minutes ticked by before Charlie said, *"I'll try once more. For both of you. If Charity could do this, I can too."*

"That's the spirit." Hope infused confidence, optimism into their link.

"Do you feel where we are in your mind?" Tony asked.

"Maybe. Connection feels tenuous."

"You have to go deeper, Hope," Tony urged.

She recalled the rampaging mess she'd found last time she plumbed Charlie's mind. Fear tightened her guts into a host of writhing snakes.

A new energy joined them. Honor.

"We can do this," she said. *"I've been listening in, auditing.*

"Charlie. I'm here too," Honor said. *"We're going to move deeper into your mind. When you sense all of us, sing out."*

Hope pressed deeper, a millimeter at a time, waiting for a path to show itself before proceeding.

"Now," Charlie said. *"Now."*

"This won't make a whole lot of sense," Tony cautioned, *"but latch onto our kinetics. It's a metaphorical latching, but it will work. Let us pull you back."*

"I'm there, best as I can. Do it," Charlie shouted.

He sounded so much like the old Charlie, Hope could've cried. Instead, she let Tony guide their joined energy through layers of Charlie's mind. It took far longer than she'd anticipated, which told her how deep they'd been and how far Charlie had sunk.

"Hang on," Tony exhorted. *"Almost there, but this last part is critical. The fiends that want to drag you down will fight like hell to hang onto you."*

Almost as if Tony's words were prophetic, Charlie's face contorted into a rictus and an ungodly scream emerged. It sounded as if he were being ripped in two.

"Keep going," Frank urged and closed a hand hard around Hope's wrist.

"But he's in pain," she protested.

"Better than being dead or lost in a place he'll never return from. Keep going. You have one chance, and it's now. He's not strong enough for you to do this again."

Hope squeezed her eyes shut and visualized Charlie. His hold on their joined kinetics had weakened, so she wrapped strands around the shiny parts that were his essence trying its damnedest to return to the life he'd known. Other strands joined hers, and she recognized Honor and Tony's energy.

Her muscles corded into rocks and she heard herself panting in great, heaving gasps, but it was working. Between Charlie clawing himself toward the surface and them dragging him, they were winning.

"Jesus. What the holy fuck?" Roy's voice boomed from somewhere behind her.

Hope ignored it. Almost. They were so close. Biting hard on her lower lip, she put everything she had into one last, mighty backward heave. Frank hadn't been kidding about it being their only chance to get this right. Charlie wouldn't be the only one who didn't have enough juice for another round.

Dampness sheened her cheeks. At first she thought it was sweat, but then she recognized tears. A popping sound like a vacuum releasing sent her staggering backward. Frank caught her before she went to her knees.

"Fuck! We were so close and we lost him," she groaned.

"Open your eyes, Hope," Frank commanded. "We did not lose him. You did it."

Her eyes flashed open, but she couldn't bear to look toward the bed. For once, a Nameless One had gotten things wrong. "No. You weren't there," she insisted. "I felt the connection break. He yanked out of our hold. Dammit! I tried so hard. I—"

"Hope. I'm back." Charlie's voice was weak, but clear. "Frank's right. You and Tony and Honor dragged me through something out of *Dante's Inferno*, but it worked."

"The fix should be permanent," Tony said. "I made sure of that as we withdrew. That was my job. Cleaning up the damage and setting things right."

Hope lifted her head and looked at Charlie, not believing what she'd heard. He was still flat on his back, but he was smiling and his eyes brimmed with a complex array of emotions. In their depths, she read how much she meant to him.

Frank let go of her, and she made her way to Charlie, unsure if her legs were up to the short distance. Perching on the edge of the narrow bed, she grasped his hand, noticed the leather band, and unbuckled the restraint.

"I'll get the rest of the shackles." Milton's voice was gruff. "And then we'll all clear out of here."

Hope looked for Honor and Tony, settling her gaze on each of them in turn. "Thank you. The words are inadequate, but thank you so much."

"What are sisters for?" Honor hugged her from one side. "Told you we'd pull him through."

Milton sent a pointed glance at Honor. "I ordered you not to—"

"Save it for your troops." Honor sent a sunny smile skittering toward the man she loved. "They needed me. Frank would've been overkill."

The Nameless One snorted laughter. "All the women tell me that."

Roy moved to Charlie's other side and gripped his hand. "Welcome back, dude. You're not allowed to check out. I've lost too many of my friends to freaks. Speaking of which, I want a full report about what exactly happened— when you're up to it."

"My pleasure." Charlie squeezed Roy's hand. "You'd have it right now if I weren't so trashed."

"I can wait." Roy let go and straightened. "I'm off to let Glory know the good news."

"Be sure to tell Faith and Charity." Hope nodded his way.

Roy snapped off a mock salute. "On it."

"Charity already knows. She's been nagging me telepathically." Tony grabbed a cart handle and pushed it toward the door with Frank walking next to him.

"Hold up there." Dr. Thomas unfolded himself from where he'd been leaning against one wall.

"Yes?" Frank turned toward the doctor and furled his brows in a typical Nameless One expression. His look reflected short-tempered, condescending tolerance for lesser creatures.

"You two are coming with me," the doctor stated.

"Why would we do that?" Frank asked.

"Because I'm ordering you to," Milton cut in.

"I want a detailed explanation of what just happened in here." The doctor looked from Frank to Tony and gestured toward the phalanx of telemetry monitors. "Everything is normal."

"You won't believe us," Frank said. "So what's the point?"

"I have a surprisingly open mind—for an M.D," Dr. Thomas countered in a chilly tone.

"Least you can do," Milton growled at Frank. "You commandeered his lab and took over one of his patients."

"Fine. Where do you want to have this conversation?" Tony cut in smoothly.

"My office. Leave the cart in the hall. Someone will see it gets back to the lab." Dr. Thomas strode out of the room. After exchanging eye-rolling glances, Frank and Tony followed him.

"Good to have you back, son." Milton squeezed Charlie's shoulder.

"Good to have rejoined the living, sir. I'll be back online in no time."

Milton angled his head and squinched his face into a scowl. "I remember after I had Cortexiphan. That shit packs quite a wallop. Allow yourself a few days before you expect a hundred percent."

"Come on." Honor headed for the door. "Let's give them a little time alone."

"It's what I'd planned all along." Milton followed Honor, closing the door behind them.

Hope had never let go of Charlie's hand, and she tightened her grip. He scooted to the far side of the hospital bed. "Any chance I could get you to lie next to me?"

Her heart took flight. "Pretty damn good one. Are you sure I won't hurt you?"

"Yeah, but even if you did, it'd be worth it. Come here, Hope." A husky catch in his voice betrayed suppressed emotion.

She released his hand and arranged herself on her side next to him, loving the way he felt against her. He wrapped his arms around her and she hugged him back, nestling her head into the hollow of his collarbone. Words caught just at the edge of her throat. She wasn't used to revealing her feelings any more than he was, but she was damned if a shred of discomfort would stop her.

"I'm so grateful you gathered yourself for one last try," she murmured. "It would've been a lonely life here without you. We're new talking to each other about this, but I've wanted to be yours for a long time. Even spent time imagining what it would be like to have you hold me in your arms."

"Kind of like this?"

"Exactly like this."

He cradled her head in one hand. "I'm hedging. Substituting banter because it's hard for me to say what's in my heart, but I've longed for you too. Wanted to spend time with you. Get to know you. Make love with you. Have a life with you."

"We can do all those things."

"Are you sure you still want me?" His voice cracked with embarrassment.

She pulled back so she could look at him. "Of course I do. Why would you even ask?"

"Because you saw me when I was weak and had given up." His direct hazel gaze scuttled away.

"Home is one place you don't have to be a warrior," she said.

He screwed his face into a scowl. "Yeah, but Frank and Tony and Milton and maybe Roy all saw me wimp out. Honor too. She was inside my head when I said I didn't want to try because I was done with hurting."

"You did try, though. And you hung on no matter how bad it got. When you started screaming, I would've quit except Frank told me I had to keep going, because none of us would have enough energy to try again."

"Screaming? Aww Jesus, I screamed? This just gets worse and worse. It's not as if I were injured."

Hope laid a hand on the side of his face, feeling whiskers graze her palm. "I saw nothing but respect and relief in everyone's minds. Screaming is allowed when you hurt." She turned his head so he had to look at her. "No secrets between us. If we're going to be lovers, it means I love you on your good days and the bad ones too."

Surprise rocked through her.

"What?" His hazel gaze lit with curiosity. "Your eyes just got wide as twin moons."

"I said love, and the earth didn't open up and swallow me."

"Maybe that means it's safe for me too." He quirked a playful brow. "I love you, Hope. I love your fierceness and your determination. I love it that you didn't give up on me and walk away. I love it that you believed in me when I stopped believing in myself." He grinned crookedly. "Is that enough loves for you?"

"Nah. I want all the love talk I can get." She snuggled close again. "Sleep. When we wake up, maybe they'll let me take you home."

"Which home?"

"Your choice. Mine or yours."

He tightened his hold on her. "Stay tuned. I'll let you know."

CHAPTER 14

Four days later

Charlie glanced around the table in the dining hall. They'd pushed three together to make space for all eleven of them. Hope sat by his side, her leg pressed against his. This was a recovery celebration—for him. Dinner had been succulent filet mignons, Caesar salads, creamy roast potatoes, and cauliflower casserole, washed down with bottles of Bordeaux and Cabernet. Pretty fancy, by dining hall standards. Everyone was waiting on dessert, which was a closely guarded surprise. He'd asked if a Playboy bunny would emerge from a flaming cake, and Milton just laughed.

Milton and Honor sat across from him. So did Roy and Glory. Tony and Charity held hands. Faith sat on Hope's other side. From time to time, she leaned close, and the two women exchanged whispered confidences. Frank sat next to Dr. Thomas, and the two chatted animatedly about something. They'd clearly found a way to bury their differences and blend their disparate worldviews. Science had spawned genetically altered humans; maybe it could bridge the differences that had driven them to open warfare.

Charlie hoped so.

He worked to retain his warrior persona, but joy was so

pervasive, it spilled from him. Maybe he shouldn't have had so much to drink, but then he let himself relax and enjoy being surrounded by old friends—and new ones. A lasting effect from the Cortexiphan was his kinetics were much stronger. He didn't have to stretch to read minds, and he couldn't wait to test the new limits of his strength and endurance.

Tomorrow. In the gym, he promised himself. *With Hope.*

They'd been inseparable since admitting their love for each other. She'd slept in his room, amid grumbles from infirmary staff, and spent all the time she wasn't working with him. Talking, sharing, reading, catching him up on everything.

He'd longed for even more freak power, and now he had it. In his secret places, he'd longed to be in love and share his life, and now he had that too. He was one lucky man, and he was well aware of it.

After lobbying hard to be released from the infirmary since yesterday morning, he'd been cleared just a few hours ago. Apparently, the medical personnel didn't totally trust Tony's assessment that Charlie was out of the woods.

More or less out of the woods.

Frank had told him the first few weeks might be nip and tuck but not to worry about it. Since Charlie and Milton were guinea pigs in the truest sense of the word, Frank was being conservative. And watchful. Charlie figured if he and Milton skated through adding Cortexiphan to the original injection series, the next thing to roll out of Frank and Tony's lab would be a more foolproof version to use on the Black Ops agents who wanted further augmentation.

The time prior to tonight's celebration had been taken up meeting with Milton and Roy. The freaks' latest salvo was attacking airports as a cover for stealing business class jets and helicopters. Once they'd stolen four, they'd made a strafing run over the CIA's Los Angeles field office, killing half a dozen agents who'd been trapped in the building when it collapsed. Because of the freaks' ability to mind link with computers, the plane that had flown into the building, exploding on impact, had been piloted remotely.

A suicide bomber with zero losses on the freak side of the house. If Charlie hadn't been appalled—and furious—he'd have been grudgingly impressed by freak ingenuity.

Frank and Tony had gathered all the Nameless Ones into a think-tank after the attack. Including the new recruits—who'd proven trustworthy so far—they now had twenty men. The group had been experimenting with ways to blend their kinetics in an attempt to unearth the next target. So far, they hadn't had any luck.

"What's your next move?" Charlie asked Frank.

He looked up from his conversation with the doctor. "Which one?"

"Figuring out the next target, so we can at least alert our agents."

"We've switched strategies."

Milton furled his brows. "I was going to say no work talk at the party, but you've got me curious. What's your new tactic?"

"We need to determine where the current headquarters is. It will have the master computer that has their game plan mapped out."

"Can you access it without going there?" Charlie asked, thinking about their last attempts to storm freak fortresses. The swamp hadn't been a barrel of laughs, and the compound in Maine—supposedly a minor outpost—had damn near killed him.

Frank drew his dark brows together. "Working on that too. At least from a theoretical perspective, with enough of us, we should be able to tap into its databanks from a distance of, say, fifty miles, or so. If we plot the kinetic parameter, raised to the twentieth power, on the X axis, and—"

"Enough." Milton held up a hand. "I get the picture."

"But you don't," Tony cut in. "Not really. You need the physics equations to fully—"

"I wouldn't understand them, son." Milton snapped his fingers.

The swinging doors leading into the kitchen flew open, and the rich scents of bananas and brown sugar filled the room. Kitchen staff bearing flaming dishes swept to the serving table. Setting the desserts down, they doused the flames and proceeded to dish the confection onto plates.

"Wow! Thank you!" Charlie turned to Milton. "How'd you know bananas flambé is my favorite dessert?"

Milton displayed a toothy, shark-eating grin. "What good are kinetics if you can't use them to unearth closely guarded secrets?"

Charlie grinned back. "Can hardly wait to try out my shiny new abilities, sir."

"So long as you don't practice on me," Milton growled, "all will be well."

"No worries on that front, boss." Charlie stood and trotted to the serving table. Scooping up two plates, he returned to his seat and placed one in front of Hope.

"Looks yummy. You could practically eat the smell," she announced before picking up a fork and digging in.

Charlie plopped into his seat, hunted for a fork, and then settled for a spoon instead. He inhaled the rich dessert and considered going back for a second helping, but decided it would be pure indulgence.

Heh! Guess a little bit of warrior is left in there somewhere.

Milton raised a snifter of port. "I'd like to propose a toast to Charlie's recovery and to all our new CIA recruits." He raised his glass. "Here's to a long and fruitful association."

"Here, here," Roy cut in. "And here's to an end to the war."

Amid a chorus of *I'll drink to that*, they clinked glasses.

"Time to pack it in," Milton announced. "Briefing at zero seven hundred in my large conference room tomorrow morning. Breakfast will be served."

Hope nudged Charlie. *"Did you ever decide whose house you want us to start our new life in?"*

"I heard that." Frank leered at them. "Can't get away with telepathy at a table full of freaks."

"Maybe not, but at least the normal humans are too polite to mention what they shouldn't have been listening in on," Hope countered.

Milton rose. "Up and gone, people. Morning always comes early." He slid into his coat, which had been tossed over the back of his chair, and helped Honor on with hers.

Everyone called, "Goodnight," and some variant of, "Glad to have you back," as they walked briskly from the room.

Charlie got up and offered his arm to Hope. They stopped at the row of hooks near the main door and got their jackets, zipping into them. Icy air blasted through when Charlie pulled the door open. He and Hope walked out of the dining hall leaning into each other.

"To answer your question," he said. "I haven't given the *whose house* question much thought. Yours is neater than mine."

She elbowed him. "I'd bet not. Is being a slipshod housekeeper your worst secret?"

He poked her back. "Not sure. It's right up there with wanting a stable full of horses and a couple dogs, though."

"Milton has a horse ranch in Montana."

"Yeah, I know, and I love it there. I was considering asking if he'd cut us loose for a week to hang out with his quarter horses, but now's not a good time. Too much going on, and I've been dead weight around here since our last mission."

"Oooh, you've been out of the action for a whopping six days."

"Five. I'm a simple man. I live for action." He stopped in the shadows of a grove of elms and pulled her into his arms, crushing his mouth down on hers. Wind howled around them and icy rain spit from the dark sky, but he didn't notice anything beyond the woman pressed against him. His cock jolted to attention, ramming against his suddenly too tight trousers.

Hope wound her arms around him and kissed him back. She bit his lower lip and teased his mouth with her tongue and lips. He sank his tongue into her mouth and she sparred with it. Even through their layers of winter clothing, he felt her nipples harden against his chest, and a throaty purr rose from the back of her throat.

They'd made out like crazy in his hospital bed, but the presence of cameras linking back to the nursing station had a dampening effect on anything beyond feverish kisses and groping each other. Wanting her, but not having her, had made him hotter than hell. Hope had turned the automatic eye so it scanned the ceiling, but a nurse had come running to reposition it. She'd smothered a knowing grin, but chided them about it being a hospital not a hotel.

Hope reached between them and curved a hand around his erection. His cock jumped against her hand. She ripped her mouth from his. "Any chance I could actually get to see what this looks like in the flesh? My imagination's been working overtime. I've looked at naked men on the Internet, but—"

Laughter bubbled from him. "How the hell did you get Internet porn here? We have techs monitoring usage, and we cut that kind of thing off as soon as we detect it."

She ran her tongue over her lower lip. "Trade secrets. I'll never tell." She squeezed his hard on lightly. "Back to my request." She grasped his zipper and worked it downward.

Charlie closed a hand over hers. "You want him to freeze solid and break off? It's cold out here, woman." He shifted his hand to the vee between her legs and pressed his palm against her vulva.

She squirmed beneath his touch. "Really? I didn't notice. Pretty damned hot from where I'm standing."

"My apartment is closer than yours," he said. Heat from her body seeped through her clothing, warming his questing fingers. "I want to see your body too, and not because I've never seen a naked woman before. You're special to me, Hope. I want to worship you, lick every inch of you, make love to you."

The quick jolt of her kinetics flashed into his mind, and a smile made her so striking he couldn't look away. "Aha! Now I know where you live." She eyed him speculatively. "Race you there?"

"What does the winner get?" His cock throbbed. It might be used to not getting much beyond a quick grope, but it didn't care for the status quo.

Her smile widened. "We get each other. Sooner." With a toss of her head, Hope took off, running full out.

He'd wanted to test his newly augmented power, and here was an opportunity. He bolted after her, delighted when he caught up without even breathing hard. His building loomed before them, and he skidded to a halt. A quick retinal scan opened the door, and he held it for her.

"Which way?" Spots of color decorated her cheeks, and her green eyes shone with anticipation.

A palm-activated scanner guarded the stairwell. Charlie tripped it, and the door popped open. One of Langley's older buildings, this one didn't have elevators. The CIA was in the process of retrofitting all of them, but a couple ended up on a back burner.

Hope scurried through the door and took the steps two and three at a time with Charlie right behind her. They ran up several flights to the fourth floor where yet one more scanner guarded the door.

"What's with all the security?" Hope asked.

"I put this one in. Welcome to my home." He pushed inward on the door. It opened to his apartment, which took up the entire top floor of the building. He bent and unlaced his boots, stepping out of them and dropping them in a heap of shoes under a coatrack.

Hope stopped dead, gazing from one side of his living room to another. "This is enormous. No other agents live up here?"

"That's right. It used to be Milton's, and I asked if I could have it when he moved into that house on the far side of the grounds. Roy didn't want it. Said it was too big, and most of the other guys on our team lived off campus.

"Darling." He unzipped her coat and pulled it off her shoulders. "We can talk about how I ended up here some other time. For now, all that matters is it's yours if you want it. Or you can keep your own apartment, and we can split our time between them. Or we can get a house off campus." He glanced at her feet. "Want to kick those shoes off?"

She unlaced her shoes, toed them off, and then walked behind him and reached for his coat. He tugged the zipper down and shrugged out of it. "Can I make you a drink or get you anything?" he asked.

"No. All I want is you." She moved so she faced him. "How do we do this? Do we undress first? Do we fall into each other's arms and deal with clothing as we run into problems with it?"

"My practical angel." He opened his arms. She walked into them and threaded hers around him. "How about if we start where we left off outside and trust everything will unfold as it should?"

Hope turned her face up, and he slashed his mouth across hers. Now that they were finally somewhere they could make love, he didn't want to wait. A primitive part of him wanted to rip her clothes off, turn her over a table, and take her.

He gave himself a good mental shake and slid his hands beneath her top, finding smooth, silky skin—and no bra. This was her first time. Before him, she'd never even kissed a man. He'd make damn good and sure to adore every delectable inch of her. She melted against him, liquid heat in his arms as she nipped his lips and teased his tongue with hers. Splaying her hands across his back, she dug her nails in and pulled him as close as they could get.

He ran his fingertips up her back, enjoying the ripple of muscle beneath her flawless skin. Her nipples turned to marbles where her breasts were mashed against his chest. Desire to see her breasts, to know what they looked like, not just how they felt, became an obsession.

Charlie pulled away from their kiss. His hands were already beneath her two layers of stretchy tops, so he pulled them over her head in one fluid movement, baring her from the waist up. Breath knotted in his throat as he stared at female perfection. Her shoulders were shapely with muscles that wound down her arms. Her skin was a lovely, rose-gold color, and her breasts perfect globes, tipped by coppery nipples that were puckered into stiff peaks.

Hope watched him, an uncertain expression on her face. "Is it—er, am I all right? You're just looking at me."

"More than all right. I'm stunned by your beauty." Charlie surged forward and filled his hands with her breasts, working the nipples between his fingers.

She pressed into him, relief streaming from her mingled with arousal. He sensed both with his heightened kinetics.

"You had me worried there for a moment." She squirmed beneath his touch. "The girls and I, sometimes we'd all touch ourselves with our minds joined. But it was always dark, and—"

Charlie's arousal, already approaching white heat, took another leap forward at the imagery. "You used to do circle jerks?"

"What's that?"

He laughed. Talking about sex had never been much of a comfort zone, and it felt good to shed his inhibitions. "Where teenage guys stand around in a circle and jack off. Whoever comes first wins, which is lousy training for later on when you want to please a woman."

Hope laughed too. "Now there's a mental picture. I bet there's way more normal human culture stuff I never ran across on the Internet." She reached beneath his pullover and maneuvered it over his head. He let go of her long enough to let his top fall to the ground. Once it was out of the way, he returned to fondling her high, firm breasts.

With a tentative finger, she traced his nipples. "Are yours sensitive too?"

"Very." Sparks shot from his nipples to his groin, and his cock grew harder still. If this kept up, he'd come before he even got his pants off.

"So long as I'm on a roll." Maybe she'd been inside his mind because she unlatched his belt and undid the fastenings of his trousers. They pooled around his ankles and he stepped out of them. Hope's gaze zeroed in on the tented front of his boxers. "Can I?"

"You don't need to ask. And you've already touched me." He let go of her and reached for the waistband of his shorts, but she batted his hands away.

"I can do this. I'm just nervous." Hope tugged at the elastic and slid his shorts past his hips, freeing his cock. It stood hard and proud, springing from its mat of dark curls. She ran a hand the length of him, inhaling audibly. "It's beautiful, in a strange kind of way." She closed an exploratory hand around him and stroked softly, tentatively.

Charlie pushed his shorts so they fell to the floor, enjoying her touch. He undid the fastenings on her khaki pants and pushed them downward. She was naked beneath them. No underwear to remove. Slender hips and a flat stomach tapered to long, shapely legs with dark hair nesting between them. He did the same thing he'd done outside, except this time, nothing lay between his hand and her body. He pressed his palm against her vulva and reached between her legs.

She quivered against him, and locked gazes. "Can we lie down? The floor is fine. Anywhere is fine." Her voice crackled with lust and promise.

Charlie wrapped one arm behind her back and swept the other beneath her knees, lifting her easily. The look of surprise on her face pleased him.

"I could've walked," she murmured.

"Another of those normal human traditions. I'm going to carry you across the threshold of my bedroom. If this were two hundred years ago, we'd jump over broomsticks, but no need to get too fancy."

"Broomsticks, huh?" She wound her arms around his neck and nuzzled him, kissing the length of his neck and tickling his earlobe with her tongue.

He walked the length of the living room and entered a hallway.

His bedroom was at the end, and he pushed the door open with a shoulder. A wave of protectiveness filled him. He'd care for the woman in his arms, lay down his life for her if it came to that.

"What a beautiful room," she said. "I love all the dark, inlaid wood."

Pleasure lit a small flame in his soul. "I did that. Woodworking is one of my passions." He placed her gently on the king-sized bed that butted against the far wall, and struck a match to light a pillar candle on one of the nightstands.

"Am I?" She gazed up at him.

"One of my passions?" At her nod, he went on, "More than a passion. I'm obsessed, charmed, captivated—"

Her full, sensual mouth spread in a smile. "Enough. Come here." She patted the bed.

Charlie lay next to her, enjoying the play of candlelight over her stunning body. He wanted her with a desperation that bordered on being bewitched, but he could wait, make this perfect for her. He kissed her, wrapping her in an embrace, and reveled in the touch of her, skin-to-skin, the full lengths of their bodies. She touched him like a blind person reading braille, searching for nuance and meaning in the planes of his body.

When she writhed and panted in his arms, clearly immersed in desire, he strung kisses down her neck until he was at breast level. He tongued one nipple, while playing with the other one, switching sides from time to time. She twisted beneath him until she'd wrapped her legs around one of his thighs, thrusting herself against him.

He wanted to hold her on the edge of climax, make things as intense as he could before she crested, but they were so new, he couldn't read her well. Instinctively, he joined her mind with his newly honed kinetics, and felt her arousal pulse and burn. His cock throbbed in time with her need, and he suckled the breast in his mouth harder.

He pressed a hand between her legs and rubbed the seat of her sensation. Her hips bucked against his hand, and he rubbed harder and then slid down her body, replacing his hand with his mouth. Her legs fell open, and he pressed two fingers into the scorching heat of her core, feeling her muscles clench around him. He moved farther inside, breaking through her membranes. She didn't flinch, so maybe she was too lost in passion to react to discomfort.

She buried her hands in his hair and pressed herself against his questing tongue. He swirled it around her nub and then sucked on her. The sucking pushed her into an orgasm. It blasted through his mind like a comet, and sharing her ecstasy thrilled him.

Hope jackknifed from beneath him and rolled him onto his back. She knelt over him and bent so she could take his cock into her mouth. The jolt of sexual energy when she closed her lips around him almost made him come, and he didn't want to. Not yet.

"Hope, darling. Kiss me, lick me, but be easy."

She dragged her long hair off his belly and looked up at him. "Why? Does this hurt you?"

"No. The opposite. It feels too good. I don't want to come this way. I want to be inside you. Do the same thing I did," he suggested. "Use kinetics to judge the effect of what you're doing."

A randy grin made her look like a modern-day Aphrodite. "Splendid idea. I should've thought of it. Lie back and let me play."

She licked the length of him, letting her tongue swirl around the tip. Next, she covered his shaft with little biting kisses that drove him half-mad with wanting her. Hope experimented alternating her hands and her mouth. At one point she reached between his legs, cupping his aching balls, but backed off when she sensed he'd come if she pursued that avenue.

He threaded his hands into her hair, loving the feel of the silky strands spilling through his fingers. She was a fast learner, pushing him almost to the point of no return and then backing off.

Finally, when he had to either come or die, he pulled from her mouth and said, "Straddle me. You'll be on top. That way, you control how fast and how deep."

Her face and chest were painted a lovely rose color from her arousal. She swung a leg over him and spread the heat of her body around him, lowering herself around his achingly hard appendage. Watching her face light with wonder at the sensations cascading through her was almost better than his own arousal.

They lasted through about twenty long, slow strokes before she fell forward, balancing herself with her arms on his shoulders as she moved faster. He closed his hands around her hips, stabilizing her body as he drove into her. Because he was still in her mind, he felt a climax seed itself deep in her belly before contractions began in her vault.

Charlie let himself go. The orgasm that had wanted out for an hour boiled from his balls and sheeted from him in blast after blast of heat. She cried out, and her shrieks mingled with feral grunts he barely recognized as his.

They stayed like that for long moments as their bodies quieted. He rolled them onto their sides with his cock still buried deep in her body. He could come again, and the possibility delighted him. Another advantage of the Cortexiphan, but he'd take it.

He stroked long, dark hair away from her face. "Was that good for you, sweetheart?"

"Amazing. The best. I had no idea how shattering sex with a partner would be. If I'd known…"

"Yes? What would you have done?"

Laughter rippled from her. "I have no idea. Nameless Ones aren't exactly sex incarnate."

"Well, I'm pleased and proud to be your first lover." Charlie hesitated, but the next words wanted out. "If I have my way, I'll be your only lover."

"What if I feel the same way about you? That I'll tear any other woman who so much as flirts with you limb from limb?" Her words were fierce, and he had no doubt she meant them.

"I want you to feel that way. We belong to each other. Now and always." His cock twitched where it was encased in her body, wanting another round. He told his body to stand down.

She tightened her muscles around him. "Can we do it again?"

"We could, but zero seven hundred is only a few hours away. We should sleep."

"We have the rest of our lives to sleep." She rolled onto her back, carrying him with her. "Make love to me one more time, and then we can sleep. Maybe." She wrapped her legs around his hips and ground her nub against his pubic bone.

"I love you." He balanced above her and withdrew ever so slowly, easing back in and enjoying every nerve ending as it shot pleasure all the way to his toes.

"I love you too. And I love this. It's better than all the birthdays and Christmases rolled into one." She butted her hips against him.

Joy ricocheted through him as he plumbed the woman spread-eagled beneath him. Tomorrow would bring its own set of problems, but for tonight, it was just him and Hope and the music their bodies made together.

CHAPTER 15

*H*ope sat on tender nether regions the next morning, shifting from butt cheek to butt cheek. Despite the soreness, the sweet ache between her legs reminded her of the wonders she'd discovered. Charlie stood in the front of the room. Whenever he glanced her way, adoration streamed from him for all to see. It was the same way Roy looked at Glory and Milton looked at Honor. If she were fair, Tony looked at Charity that way too, but Hope had always been reluctant to offer Nameless Ones points for anything.

Gonna have to get over that. Besides, Tony and Frank helped me save Charlie.

They're just like me, except a different sex.

At the word sex, she smothered a giggle and a blush. She'd pumped first Glory and then Honor and Charity about the joys of bedding a man, but their descriptions hadn't done it justice. Maybe words didn't exist that depicted the ecstasy she'd experienced the previous night...

"Hope!" Roy's voice cracked like a whip. "You haven't heard one word I've said."

Her head snapped up. "Guilty. Sorry. You were assigning roles for today."

"Indeed I was. And yours is?"

Hope shook her head. "I didn't hear."

"You'll be in the underground arena with the new women continuing their introduction to martial arts in the morning. After lunch, you'll take the five you're responsible for to the gun range and work on weapons practice."

"Got it." She nodded crisply. "I'll make certain to get the paperwork filled out too."

"We should have a solution for how to storm the freaks' mainframe by sometime this afternoon," Frank said.

"Excellent," Charlie spoke up. "Depending on where it is, we might have time to fly an aerial reconnaissance before nightfall."

"I'll keep you posted," Frank said. "If you take a chopper, I'd like to come along."

Charlie looked askance at him. "Only because you're hoping I'll let you fly."

Frank shrugged. "Yeah. That too." He shifted his gaze to Milton. "You'd said you were going to get us pilot's licenses."

"In process," Milton said gruffly. "You actually need driver's licenses too. You have your assignments. Get moving. Time waits for no agent."

Hope tipped back the last of her coffee and stood. She was on her way out of the room, but moving slowly so maybe she could catch a quick word with Charlie before they parted company for the day.

"McClaren, hold up," Milton called. "Hope. Front and center too."

She froze. Fear she thought she'd left behind at the compound soured her stomach. She hadn't done anything wrong, had she?

"Sometime today, Hope," Milton barked.

She turned and walked toward the front of the room. Charlie stood in front of Milton, but he didn't look stressed. Maybe she shouldn't jump to conclusions. Before she got to the two men, she blurted, "I'm sorry I wasn't paying attention when Roy handed out assignments. I'll do better, I promise. I have my tasks for today, and—"

"Hope. It's all right." Charlie held out a hand, and she clasped it.

Heat swooshed from her chest over the top of her head when she realized she was holding hands with Charlie—in front of Milton. She wrenched her hand back. Unable to look at either man, she studied the floor.

"What did you need from me, sir?" she mumbled.

"What did I do to make you afraid of me?" Milton's voice was kind.

She made a decision, squared her shoulders, and met his gaze head on. "Nothing. It's not you, sir. It's all the years I spent in the compound."

"I'm relieved it's not me." Milton chuckled. "I know I can be a bastard, but you looked like a waif being led to the guillotine. What I wanted was this." He glanced from her to Charlie. "McClaren, you never take time off. You have so much leave time on the books, we've been docking you for it. I want you to have at least a week longer to recover."

"Noted, but you need every seasoned agent right now." Charlie focused his hazel eyes on Milton.

A smile played around the edges of Milton's mouth. "Look, son. There's always another war. You won't miss anything critical. Besides, this isn't an option, it's an order. Take from now through next Sunday off. Leave Langley. Take Hope with you."

"But I have a job to do today," she protested.

"That you do, which means you'll leave tonight," Milton clarified. "It'll take that long for Charlie to get a few things packed, file flight plans, and do the rest of the planning to be gone for a short time. You would like a few days with your new man, wouldn't you?"

Not trusting herself to speak, Hope nodded. Milton was being beyond kind, and gratitude cascaded through her.

"In addition to mandating a vacation, have you decided where we'll be spending it?" Charlie looked askance at his boss.

Milton snorted. "You always were too smart for your own good. You have two choices. The bed and breakfast in the San Juans or my ranch in Montana. I want you safe, and I don't have men to spare to send with you."

"What do you think?" Charlie eyed Hope. "It's not just my choice."

Hope swallowed hard. She loved Charlie for putting her first. Emotion churned, turning her insides to mush. "You were talking about Milton's horse ranch last night, so how about there."

Milton furled his salt and pepper brows. "What exactly were you saying about my horse ranch?"

Charlie flashed a grin. "That I wanted one just like it someday."

"They're a lot of work," Milton cautioned, "and I don't spend nearly enough time enjoying it, but Honor and I plan to retire there."

"Retire?" Charlie stared at Milton. "Do you know something you're not sharing?"

"Not at all, son. There's a lot of life left in this old buzzard. Retirement's for somewhere down the road."

"Yeah, right. You're addicted to danger, just like me. Now that we have a location tacked down," Charlie went on. "I bet you have an idea of how we're going to get there, and it doesn't involve flying commercial."

"You'd be right," Milton replied. "Take the small Gulfstream. I'll deduct some nominal amount from your pay."

"Nominal?" Charlie looked sidelong at Milton. "Those suckers cost tens of thousands of dollars to rent."

"Special deal. Just for you. Now get moving, both of you. I have a full plate today."

"Thank you, sir. The words don't even come close, but thank you just the same." Hope held out a hand, and Milton grasped it.

"You're welcome. Take good care of Charlie."

"We'll take care of each other," Charlie said.

Hope felt his gaze on her, and heat rose to her face. She buried the blush with kinetics, but she'd have to do a smidge of reprogramming so she didn't turn red so often or so fast.

Milton released her hand. "Scoot," he repeated. "Hope, you're late for the underground practice arena. They've begun without you."

She loped out the door with Charlie behind her and headed for the nearest exit to outside. "Pick you up around six," he said. "Bring warm clothes. Montana is an icebox this time of year."

"Colder than Langley?" she turned to ask.

"Use your databank brain," he countered. "Much colder, but we'll find ways to make our own heat."

Hope mock slugged him. "Only a few hours and we'll have a whole week together. Alone."

Charlie gave her a quick, hard hug. "I know. I should feel guiltier about leaving here, but Milton's right. It's been years since I've taken leave time. I had so much on the books, they started taking it away."

"Soon." She sprinted toward the building that housed the underground arena.

"Can't wait," he called after her.

Hope let herself into the building and punched the button to call the elevator. This was the only place she ever used them, mostly because the arena was so far underground. Her heart felt light and fluttery, but now wasn't the time to daydream about Charlie and more of his kisses or the hard-muscled planes of his body kneeling above her.

Now was a time to focus.

She'd been scared for no reason when Milton singled her out leaving the conference room. She wanted to be sure not to give him any reason to be displeased with her. He'd been kind and generous, and she'd repay that with her undying loyalty.

She left the elevator and bee-lined it into the changing room to shuck her outer garments. As soon as she entered the arena, the rest of the women stopped what they were doing and headed for her, surrounding her in a rough circle.

"Well?" Honor shoved closer.

"Well, what?" Hope tried for a nonchalant expression, but every single woman in here was a freak. They could dive bomb her mind and unearth her secrets.

"You and Charlie, what else?" Glory smiled knowingly.

The heat she'd been successful diverting earlier swamped Hope, and she was certain her face matched a blood red poster tacked to one wall. "Erm. We're good," she stammered.

"Just good?" Charity waggled her eyebrows.

"Did Milton offer you time off with Charlie?" Ever direct, Honor crossed her arms beneath her breasts.

"How'd you know about that?" Hope's eyes widened.

"Because we don't have any secrets, and he asked if I thought you'd go or if it was too soon."

A smile wanted out, but Hope pressed her lips together. "So long as you were planning my future behind my back, what'd you tell him?"

"That you'd been mooning over Charlie for months," Charity cut in.

A few of the newer women leaned forward amid a collective sigh. Ooohs and aaahs rose around Hope.

"What's it like?" one asked. "Now that you finally have a man who's all your own."

Hope shook her head. "We're not going to go there. Today is a work day, and we're going to practice—just like we're supposed to."

"Are you going with Charlie?" Honor persisted.

Hope nodded. "We leave tonight. Back in a week. We'll be at Milton's ranch."

Honor's green eyes shone with enthusiasm. "You're going to love it there. It's where Milton took me—once I pulled my head out of my ass and admitted how special he was to me."

Faith squeezed through the crowd and wrapped her arms

around Hope. "I'm happy for you," she said. "Even if it means I'm the last of us to not find the love of her life."

"You will," Hope assured her.

Faith shrugged. "I don't know. It seems impossible."

"What seems impossible?" Glory pushed forward and draped an arm around Faith's shoulders.

"I'm not going to say anything more." Faith turned away from Hope and Glory and ran to the far side of the arena.

"Do you have any idea who she's sweet on?" Glory asked, keeping her voice low.

Hope shook her head. "I have a feeling if we watch really close, we'll find out, though."

Laughter rippled from Glory. "True enough." She clapped her hands. "Back to your groups, everyone. Let's make the CIA proud of us."

After today, Hope wanted Milton to be proud of her. His actions had cemented her devotion to the CIA. He was a good commander. The best, in her book. Compassion mixed with toughness were traits he shared with his handpicked group of men.

Charlie flashed across her mind, and her heart beat a little faster. Soon, very soon, they'd be in one another's arms. Anticipation began in her toes and raced all the way to the top of her head in a tingly rush.

"Coming?" Honor beckoned with one hand.

"You betcha!" Hope ran lightly to the small group of women who'd been assigned to her. "Mind meld," she instructed. "Let's try to be more elegant—and faster—than we were yesterday."

"Who will teach us while you're gone?" one of the women asked.

"I don't know, but I'll be back before you know it." Hope let her gaze settle on each woman in turn. "You're new, and it's hard to trust this will be a safe haven, but it is. The CIA will value and care for you. Enough jabbering. Join my kinetics now."

Hope threw her mind wide open and felt the others braid their mental power with hers. It gave her hope for the future of their kind. And for a time when normal humans and freaks would fight on the same side. The world was full of battlegrounds, and they were stronger working together. Wasting resources killing each other because the Nameless Ones were immersed in a years' old grudge match was illogical and shortsighted.

She smiled grimly. She'd chided the others about focus, and hers was wandering. Strengthening her links with the other women, Hope began the day's exercises.

You've reached the end of *Loving Hope*. Book five of *GenTech Rebellion*, *Keeping Faith*, will be along very soon. Read on for a sample.

ABOUT THE AUTHOR

Ann Gimpel is a USA Today bestselling author. A lifelong aficionado of the unusual, she began writing speculative fiction a few years ago. Since then her short fiction has appeared in a number of webzines, magazines, and anthologies. Her longer books run the gamut from urban fantasy to paranormal romance to science fiction. Once upon a time, she nurtured clients. Now she nurtures dark, gritty fantasy stories that push hard against reality. When she's not writing, she's in the backcountry getting down and dirty with her camera. She's published more than 50 books to date, with several more planned for 2018 and beyond. A husband, grown children, grandchildren, and wolf hybrids round out her family.

Keep up with her at www.anngimpel.com or http://anngimpel.blogspot.com

If you enjoyed what you read, get in line for special offers and pre-release special reads. Sign up for Ann's newsletter on her website or her blog.

KEEPING FAITH, CHAPTER ONE

Faith walked slowly across Langley's campus. She'd just seen Hope and Charlie off at the terminal building next to the airstrip. They'd looked deliriously happy, and Faith was grateful Charlie's near miss with death hadn't left lasting problems. She stuffed her hands into her pockets, wishing she'd brought gloves. For once it wasn't raining, but it was almost dark.

Milton Reins, head of the CIA, had been there to wish Hope and Charlie well too. He'd also been chockful of instructions about the Gulfstream business class jet until Charlie reminded his boss that he was qualified to fly that particular plane.

Not quite ready to return to her apartment building and all the new women who'd been assigned housing there, Faith wandered aimlessly. Glory, Honor, Charity, and Hope—women who were like sisters to her—had hooked up with men they loved dearly. A few months back, they'd lived in a compound in Washington State with seven more genetically modified women just like them. Glory's bravery freed them, and Faith blessed the CIA every single day for taking a chance on them as agents.

More women had joined their ranks during a raid they'd just completed in Maine. Twenty to be precise. It made her heart glad the women had been able to lay their reservations aside and take a chance on a new life. One where they'd be treated like human beings, rather than slaves.

She really should hustle back to the apartment building and see if any of them wanted to go to dinner. Faith remembered her first days at Langley. How lost and overwhelmed she'd felt. It had helped Glory was already there. The least she could do was pass on the goodwill to the new gals.

"Faith. Hold up."

She glanced over her shoulder at the sound of Frank's voice, but kept walking. Frank was genetically modified too, but he'd been one of the Nameless Ones, men who'd made the women's life holy hell in the compounds. He was also a genetic researcher. Her friend Charity had fallen in love with Tony, the scientist Frank had defected with, but it didn't mean Faith harbored fond feelings for any of the genetically modified men.

During the seven years the CIA had hunted them, they'd labeled them freaks. The tag stuck, and she still thought of men like Frank as freaks, but not necessarily her or the women.

How's that for hypocrisy? She smothered a snorting laugh.

"What's so funny?" Frank caught up with her.

Faith shrugged. I was thinking about how the CIA calls us freaks, and I'm good when it means you. Less good when it means me."

"Doesn't matter what they call us," Frank countered. "They took us in. Gave us homes and work. They didn't have to. How'd Charlie look? I'd meant to check him over one last time before he left, but didn't get there in time."

"Like the old Charlie. None the worse for wear. Dr. Thomas was there. I'm pretty sure he had some of the same concerns you do, but Milton told him to go back to his infirmary."

Frank hooted laughter. "Bet that didn't go over very well."

"No. It didn't. The doc stayed until Charlie and Hope headed out onto the tarmac." Faith narrowed her eyes. "You've gotten to know him pretty well, huh?"

"Who?"

"The doctor."

"In a manner of speaking, yeah. After Tony and I pulled a rabbit out of a black hole and saved Charlie, the guy decided we weren't just a bunch of uninformed quacks pretending we knew something about physiology."

"You're mixing your metaphors."

"So?" Frank angled his unusual amber eyes with their vertical slit pupils her way. Like all the genetically modified men, he was tall and broad-shouldered with a rangy build. Unevenly cut jet-black hair hung to his shoulders.

"So, nothing. Just pointing it out. Um, did you want something? I really should get back to the apartment building. We have all those new women, and—"

"Yeah I did," he interrupted in true Nameless One fashion.

Faith shook off irritation. "Whatever it is, spit it out."

He tucked a hand beneath her elbow in a distressingly familiar gesture. "How about joining me in the cafeteria for dinner? Tony and I got done early tonight, and he's spending the night in with Charity."

Faith jerked away from his touch. "The new women are my first responsibility," she said stiffly, wishing Frank would take the hint and leave. If he were human, he might've, but subtlety and picking up on social cues weren't part of how any of them had been programmed.

"Bring 'em along." He grinned rakishly. "You may not like me, but one of them might."

Faith stopped walking and stared at him. "What the hell, Frank? Any woman in a storm?"

"Now who's mixing metaphors?" He looked down his nose at her.

Faith felt her face heat. "I'll be in the dining hall in half an hour or so. If you want to sit with us, that's fine—so long as none of the women object. They're much fresher from a compound than me, so they may well run screaming from the room if you get too close."

Frank closed a hand around one wrist, effectively trapping her. "Get real, Faith. I wasn't in your compound, but it wasn't as if we flogged the women. You make it sound as if we were the devil incarnate."

"To us, you were. You rationed everything from food to blankets to when we had to show up to have our eggs harvested." She angled her head to one side. "The men in my compound ate what they wanted. They weren't half-starved like us. I bet they had more than one blanket. And they had private rooms; they weren't stuffed twelve to a dorm like we were—"

"You can stop now." Frank held up his other hand. "I'm sorry. I felt bad at the time I didn't do more, and I still do, but you living in the past and hanging onto hostility and bitterness isn't wise."

"Why not?" she demanded. "What's the phrase? He who forgets history is doomed to repeat it."

"George Santayana said that, but you're living in a different world now. The odds are better than seventy percent that the CIA will effectively quell the rebellion sometime in the next six months. V4 has proven unstable. God only knows how many freaks were made with that configuration, but they'll implode, which will further thin their ranks."

"Fascinating," she muttered, "but I need to get moving."

Frank released her wrist. "I'd like to get to know you better, Faith, but I won't be heavy-handed about it. Give it some thought and let me know."

She took a step backward. "What about wanting to give the women a thrill by having dinner with them?"

"Eh, I just said that to see if you'd react. Be jealous or something." He actually looked mildly uncomfortable when he twisted his mouth into a frown. "You weren't, and I'm crushed, but I'll get over it."

Without waiting for a response from her, he spun and took off at a quick lope.

Faith ran hard the other way, heading for her apartment building. Her thoughts were a roiling mess. Charity may have managed to square hooking up with a nameless one, but Faith didn't have it in her to overlook their years of horrific treatment. They may not have been beaten, but they'd endured every other type of abuse.

Except sexual.

Intimacy was forbidden in the compounds. The reason Glory had run away was because a Nameless One tried to rape her. She'd used her kinetics to kill him, been scared half to death, and gone out a window in the thick of winter with only a worn pair of tennis shoes and a threadbare sweater. It was hard enough in Washington, but by the time she'd hitchhiked halfway across the country to Minnesota, the cold had almost killed her.

Frank was a hunk of a man. All the Nameless Ones were, but Faith couldn't see herself letting her guard down long enough to let him inside her hopes and dreams, let alone sleeping with him. The thought made her vaguely ill.

She reached her building and tipped her chin so the retinal scanner could trip the lock and let her in. She was capable of employing kinetics to spring any lock, but so long as she was here, she'd do things the CIA way. After she nodded to the guard patrolling the lobby, she pulled open a stairwell door and headed for the third floor.

Faith employed telepathy as she hastened up the stairs to see which women might be interested in joining her for dinner in the cafeteria. By the time she got to her floor, seven of the new recruits waited for her, milling about in the hallway. Faith recognized three of them since they were part of a group assigned specifically to her for weapons and martial arts practice.

A thought struck Faith. "I never asked, and we mostly

communicate via telepathy when we train, but did you ever swap out your identification numbers from the compounds for names?"

A woman from Faith's group squared her shoulders. Like all the genetically modified women, she had long, thick dark hair and clear green eyes. The women had sleekly muscled bodies, and were both tall and strong. "Some of us did," she replied.

Faith smiled grimly. "That was one of the concessions we insisted on in my compound. We got sick of numbers, so we named ourselves and refused to respond when Nameless Ones called us by our numbers. Tell you what. Before we're done eating tonight, at least the seven of you will have picked names."

"Sounds like a plan," another of the women said.

"Tell us about Hope and Charlie," another pressed forward and clasped her hands together. "It seems like such a fairytale romance. Everything went well? They're off on a honeymoon?"

"Well, they're not exactly married, so honeymoon isn't the correct word," Faith replied. "But I watched their plane take off, and they did look happy."

A collective *ahhhhh* surged through the group, and seven pairs of green eyes shone with delight for one of their kind who'd found happiness.

Faith could relate, and it made her both sad and angry. Up until she'd fled the compound, the thought of falling in love was just a fantasy. Something that happened in movies she watched on the Internet, but nothing that would ever happen to her. Frank's invitation—and his obvious interest—nagged at the back of her mind.

No. I'd rather be dead than hook up with a Nameless one. Charity may have, but I'm not her.

"Dinner?" Faith urged to quell her churning thoughts and trotted back down the stairway. If they got there after eight, the steam tables would be closed. Snacks were always available, but they weren't as satisfying as a hot meal.

The women trailed after her, chatting among themselves. They sounded carefree, another emotion that had eluded them in the compounds where they'd had to watch their backs every single minute.

"What do you think about goddess warrior names?" One of the women joined Faith.

"It doesn't matter what I think," Faith offered. "A name is important. It symbolizes who you are. Humans don't get to pick their own names, but some of the research I've read indicates that people grow into their given names—for good or for ill."

"So I should pick a name where I have an affinity for the woman, right?"

"Sounds good to me," Faith replied. "In our compound, we picked simple names that had meaning for us. We figured if we selected anything too complicated, we'd never get the men to quit hollering out our numbers when they wanted something."

Another woman closed on Faith's other side. "Was it easy?" she asked.

"The transition?" Faith glanced her way.

"Yeah. How long did it take them to give up and use names?"

Faith buried a snort. "Some got on the bandwagon in six months. Took others a year. And they cut our rations and assigned us extra duties to force us to give up on having names. We held firm, though. It was our first victory, and we wrangle every last bit of pleasure we could out of it."

"The men don't have names." Someone spoke up.

"Yeah, they do. They just never used them around us. One guy slipped up. It was what gave us the impetus to demand names for ourselves." Faith slapped her palm on the reader plate outside the cafeteria and pushed the door open.

"Get your food," she instructed, "and we'll push a couple of tables together. In fact, I'll do that while you're in line, so the table will be ready."

Amid repeated *thank yous*, Faith strode to the back of the large room. All the tables seated four, so she pushed three together. That done, she stopped by the drink table for a cup of coffee and left it in front of her place before crossing to the steam tables lined up at the far end. The cafeteria had zero ambience, but it served good food under the harsh glare of banks of fluorescent panels.

By the time she slid into her seat, the other women were already eating.

One set her fork down and smiled self-consciously. "This—" she waved a hand expansively around the table at the overflowing plates "—feels like more of a miracle than anything else. We never, never had enough food."

Faith remembered all too well. "At least that part of our lives is over—I hope," she murmured and began to eat.

Other women from the Maine compound filtered in, and Faith pushed more tables in line with theirs.

"What happens with practice tomorrow?" one of the women who'd been on Hope's team asked.

"Well, out of the five of you assigned to Hope, two will come with me, and three with Charity for the week Hope is gone."

Faith did a quick nose count. All but two of the women from Hope's group were there, and they'd been assigned to Charity. "You two—" she pointed "—will be with me and my five. And you—" she pointed again "—will join Charity."

"Which one is she?" the woman asked.

The woman sitting next to her leaned close. "The one who hooked up with a Nameless One."

"Ohhh." A knowing look creased the first woman's face. "I know who she is."

Faith licked dry lips. She should keep quiet, but a need to speak up for her friend won out. "Charity is amazing. You're lucky to have her for an instructor. She's one of the V3s with an unstable genome, but she got past it by being one strong bitch of a woman."

"But a Nameless One…" The woman who'd asked the question looked at her plate.

"Charity had a hell of a hard time swallowing that," Faith said.

"But Tony saved her when her genome hit a downward spiral, and he adores her."

"I suppose it's possible," a woman on Faith's team muttered, "but it kind of makes my skin crawl."

Murmured assent rose from several women.

"Names." Faith changed the subject. "You all need to pick names —unless you already have them." She stabbed her fork into china and realized her plate was empty. The abrupt motion told her how difficult the conversation about Tony and Charity was for her to hear, let alone be part of. It brought Frank's earlier invitation front and center again too.

She pushed to her feet. "I'm going to call it a night. You can remain here as long as you want. No one will kick you out of the cafeteria. For those of you on my team, we'll meet at zero eight hundred sharp in the underground arena. Unless we receive other orders between now and then. If that happens, I'll alert you myself."

Faith loped toward a door and snapped her coat off a hook, sliding into it as she walked out the door. She kept her head down, mostly so she wouldn't have to think about anything, and plowed right into Dr. Thomas.

Faith halted abruptly. "I— I'm sorry," she muttered. "Wasn't watching where I was going."

"It's all right, Faith." The doctor smiled pleasantly. His dark hair was shorn close to his head and he had green eyes, but a darker shade than hers. Tall and thin, he'd been a field surgeon in the Middle East. He was the one who'd pitched nine kinds of fits about Frank and Tony treating Charlie, but to his credit, he'd backpedaled fast.

Hard to argue with success, and the doctor hadn't tried.

He was still gazing at her. It made her uncomfortable, so she studied him to give herself something to do. She was used to collecting data with her computer-esque brain. He'd tossed a fur-lined coat over scrubs and was probably intent on dinner.

"So long as I ran into you—rather literally it turns out—I've been meaning to ask you something," He quirked an inquisitive brow her way.

Faith thinned her mouth into an aggravated line. What was it about men and asking her things tonight? "I'm waiting." She ditched her discomfort and latched her gaze onto his before she remembered humans didn't appreciate that level of directness.

"You have some good skills. I've seen you patch the women up when they get hurt in the arena. Did you do any work in the labs in your compound?"

"Not the labs, but I did do some medical support work, why?" Before he could answer, she hurried on. "I really enjoy field work, uh, sir. Not sure I'd want to be stuck in someplace like the infirmary all day. Not that it isn't nice and all—" Faith realized she was blithering and cut off her flow of words. She'd take whatever tasks the CIA assigned. To do anything else would be the height of ingratitude.

"Stop by the infirmary tomorrow," he said. "Say around noon. That shouldn't interrupt your morning training schedule. I've been extremely impressed with Frank and Tony's knowledge base, and I have an idea I'd like to float past you."

"I'm not a Nameless One," she mumbled.

"Oh yes, that is what you women call them, isn't it." He smiled again. "See you tomorrow, Faith. I'm looking forward to our chat."

Reginald Thomas touched his palm to the scanner and disappeared inside, leaving Faith staring after him.

She forced her gaze away from watching him through the glass door and turned toward her apartment building. Efforts to keep her mind blank failed. Where Frank's invitation had creeped her out, the doctor's fascinated her. Was he interested in her as something other than some kind of guinea pig? A hybrid type of medical personnel who could think outside of standardized training?

Her heart gave a funny little flutter, and her statement about preferring fieldwork hit the skids. She'd give up weapons practice, telepathy skills enhancement, and martial arts workshops in a hot minute if it meant she got to spend her days next to Dr. Thomas.

"Oh, put a lid on it," Faith muttered and walked into her building.

"What was that, miss?" the security guard asked.

"Nothing. Just talking to myself. Good evening, Greg."

"And a good evening to you as well, Miss Faith."

She took the stairs three at a time and ran down the hall to her apartment, letting herself in. Faith paced in circles for a long five minutes before engaging her kinetics. She'd be in big trouble if she were caught, but she was determined to hack into the CIA's personnel database and find out everything she could about Reginald Thomas.

I'll stop the minute I find a wife, she promised herself, but wondered if she'd be disciplined enough to quit there.

www.ingramcontent.com/pod-product-compliance
Lightning Source LLC
Chambersburg PA
CBHW071301190726
48292CB00007B/2634